D1553420

ANTHONY RYAN

This special signed edition is limited to 1000 numbered copies and 26 lettered copies.

This is copy 853.

TO BLACKFYRE KEEP

THE SEVEN SWORDS

Book Four

Anthony Ryan

Subterranean Press • 2022

Edited by Yanni Kuznia

First Edition

ISBN
978-1-64524-085-3

Subterranean Press
PO Box 190106
Burton, MI 48519

subterraneanpress.com

Manufactured in the United States of America

To that most insightful modern prophet of doom, and originator of ambulatory corpse tropes, George A. Romero.

Some who claim wisdom will advise that we must embrace death
For death is but part of the eternal circle.
They are wrong.
Death must be shunned.
Death must be denied.
Death must be despised and fought with every last mote of strength we possess.
For in embracing death, you reject life,
The only true gift you will ever receive.

—*Injunctions of the First Risen.*

Chapter One

The Stone Bears

Guyime was no stranger to the icy caress of befogged mountain air, although it had been many years since he felt such a bone-deep chill. *Cold and damp, damp and cold,* Lakorath said in a doleful mutter, words that had become something of a mantra for the demon as the northlands loomed ever closer. *I confess, my liege, I remain baffled why you and your fellow barbarians were so intent on killing each other for possession of so miserable a land.* The sword on Guyime's back shifted as its inhabitant exuded an uncharacteristic if muted thrum of wistful nostalgia. *Give me the sulphur dunes of the Tormenting Plain any day. Or the acid waves of the Incubus Ocean. Now there's a sweet aroma.*

"Sounds delightful," Guyime returned in a sigh, pausing at the crest of the ridge they had spent much of the morning climbing. He assumed the mountains that stretched away to east and west would have made an impressive sight when viewed from such a vantage point. However, the mist swirled in thick shifting banks around them, the obscuring clouds becoming more dense the higher they climbed.

Guyime unhitched the water flask from his belt and drank deep. "Makes me wonder why you ever chose to depart the Infernus at all," he added, squinting at the occluded landscape ahead and seeing nothing beyond anonymous, mist-shrouded rock.

Chose is not the right word, Lakorath said, his tone taking on a peevish edge. *Lured by vile mortal perfidy is far closer to the mark.*

"It occurs to me," Guyime said, "that you have never told me the full tale of how you came to be trapped in that sword."

Lakorath, in a yet more uncharacteristic display, said nothing in response to this pointed observation. Throughout the many years of their binding, this subject remained the only one the demon refused to discuss beyond vague allusions to the untrustworthiness of mortal kind. It served as a useful means of shutting the creature up when his acerbic prattle or dark encouragements grew tiresome, but considering their current mission, Guyime found his unwanted companion's reticence increasingly intolerable.

"I'll have it from you," he promised Lakorath, glancing over his shoulder at the sword's hilt. "And soon."

Lakorath, once again, said nothing and the sword remained an unmoving length of metal on Guyime's back.

Letting out a grunt of restrained frustration, Guyime turned to survey the progress of the rest of the party in scaling the ridge. Predictably, Seeker was in the lead. Despite the unfamiliarity of the climate and the weight of the caracal she carried in a sling across her chest, the beast charmer displayed typical fortitude and resilience in traversing these peaks. Lissah, by contrast, was in a far more distressed state than her mistress, giving voice to a constant string of mewling complaints. Guyime couldn't tell if the caracal's agitation stemmed from the cold or the constricting annoyance of the sling. Seeker had resorted to carrying the cat in a blanket of fox furs when it became apparent the frigid air was making the beast both lethargic and unpredictably vicious.

Evidence of Lissah's fractious temper came in the form of the bandage covering the back of Lorweth's hand. He was next in line behind Seeker, climbing with long-legged confidence that told of a familiarity with high places and little concern for the chill. The druid's mood had actually seemed to improve upon entering the mountains, the caustic note that usually coloured his many attempts at wit giving way to occasional displays of genuine cheeriness. This had dimmed somewhat when Lissah lashed out to score a series of deep scratches in Lorweth's hand. The Mareth had made an unwise attempt to pet her when they clustered around the previous night's campfire. Still, today he climbed with an expression of contented surety which Guyime supposed arose from finding himself in a region so similar in climate to the Mareth homeland.

Lexius exhibited no such contentment. Even though the scholar's eyes were distorted by the thick lenses he wore, Guyime still saw the fatigue in the diminutive man's gaze. Even so, he continued to bear his pack without complaint and maintained a dogged if plodding pace on the slope. As he walked Lexius spoke in a low murmur, Guyime divining he was engaged in continual conversation with the inhabitant of his own sword. The Kraken's Tooth hung at his side, the occasional glow of the blade becoming noticeable when the light grew dim. Guyime resolved to advise the scholar against conversing so openly with the spirit of his slain wife when they next found themselves in more mundane company.

Orsena had positioned herself at the rear of their party since commencing this sojourn into the northern peaks. Guyime knew it had nothing to do with a lack of fortitude, since the Ultria of House Carvaro could most likely continue walking to the ends of the earth without need of sustenance or rest. She had discovered this aspect of her unique physicality when they first set out from Atheria. Having awoken to her true nature as a magically animated statue, Orsena opted to forgo eating or drinking for several days. Whilst she grew notably more irritable and reported severe pangs of hunger, she lost no weight nor faltered in a single step.

"Why?" she had wondered aloud to Guyime at the end of their first week on the road north. "Why afflict me with hunger when I don't need to eat?"

"You were never meant to know what you are," Guyime reminded her. "That was your father's... Ultrius Carvaro's intention."

Mention of the man Orsena had thought her father invariably drew her features into an expression that Guyime felt to be the closest she would come to ugliness. "Sometimes I feel I should thank Temesia for killing him," she said, a bitter edge to her voice. "For it spared me the burden."

Watching the way Orsena scaled the ridge, Guyime saw that her apparent slowness resulted from her habit of halting now and then to take in her surroundings. Such pauses had also been a frequent vice of hers during their trek through the farmland north of the City of Songs. Despite all the knowledge with which she had been imbued, the memories of the murdered woman she resembled, he knew Orsena to be a soul seeing the world at large for the first time. In many ways, she remained a child, an innocent compelled to follow the most hazardous path. The notion stirred a protective urge alongside the guilt that arose from including her in this grand but most likely fatal mission.

You could have left her behind, Lakorath pointed out. *Spared her all the horrors to come. For you know there will be horrors, don't you, my liege?*

"She bears one of the demon-cursed blades," Guyime replied. "There is nowhere else for her to be."

His gaze slipped to the curve-bladed short sword in the scabbard hanging from Orsena's belt. Unlike Lexius, she felt no compulsion to talk to the blade's inhabitant. However, from the occasional winces and frowns that passed across the Ultria's unnaturally symmetrical features, Guyime divined the demon imprisoned in the Conjurer's Blade felt no such reluctance.

"What's it saying to her?" he asked Lakorath, drawing a snort of indifferent disdain.

I stopped listening weeks ago, the demon informed him. *She's dreadfully tedious, I'm afraid, and so pretentious. Prates on endlessly about all things artistic or architectural.*

"She?" Guyime asked in surprise. "You referred to it as a he before."

Yes. Lakorath's response was tinged with scorn at his wielder's mortal ignorance. *Demons are changeable creatures, my liege. Sometimes male, sometimes female, sometimes neither, or both if the mood takes us. Gender is a mortal conceit we adopted for our amusement. The arch-bore residing within the Conjurer's Blade prefers to match the nature of its wielder.*

"And does this she-demon have a name?"

Not one I've discerned, as yet. My kind is always very circumspect in sharing such things.

This, at least, Guyime knew to be true. He hadn't learned the name of the creature he was bound to until it had been spoken by the Mad God. In truth, it occurred to him that much of the information he possessed about demon-kind had only been garnered since he embarked upon his mission to find the Seven Swords. To claim them, he would need to acquire more.

"What is that?" Seeker said, halting as she came to his side atop the ridge. Her face, no longer bearing the monochrome paint that had once masked it, narrowed in careful scrutiny of the next rise. Following her gaze, Guyime saw a large shape revealed by a thinning of the mist some fifty paces off. It remained a vague, formless slab of twelve-foot-high stone in the haze, but he knew it of old.

"The first of the Stone Bears," he said, starting forward.

As the statue came fully into view, Guyime was struck by the scant changes it had suffered in the many years since he last passed this way. It was weathered and cracked in places but still recognisable as a representation of a rearing bear. Its maw gaped to reveal large, curved fangs, granite lips drawn back in a snarl.

"Is it a marker, my lord?" Lexius enquired as he and Lorweth joined them. The scholar's distorted eyes lost much of their fatigue as he peered up at the stone beast with his usual unquenchable curiosity. "A signifier that we are now in the Northern Kingdom?"

"Many take it as such," Guyime replied, his gaze shifting from the statue to scan the surrounding slopes. "But the Stone Bears were originally raised as a warning."

"Trying to scare of southern invaders, eh?" Lorweth said.

"No." Guyime quelled a grimace of annoyance at the obscuring vapour all around. "They tell travellers what they're likely to encounter if they climb high into these peaks."

"You mean…" Lorweth's handsome features tensed as he looked again at the statue. "This? There are bears this size nearby?"

"The proportions are exaggerated, but not by much."

Seeker angled her head to peer up at the bear's snarling maw. "I know not this breed," she said. "And it's rare for bears to live in high places."

"They're a rare sort, to be sure," Guyime told her. "Legend tells of a mage using the ancient bones of a long-extinct creature to raise up an army of bears to fight a battle in the latter stages of the Kraken Wars. Supposedly, when the battle was done and their master slain, the bears took to the mountains where they remain to this day, subsisting on goats and the occasional unfortunate traveller."

Guyime's gaze lingered on Seeker, brows raised in a question. The beast charmer had a peerless sense for natural dangers, although she hadn't seen fit to unlimber her bow as yet. "I sense nothing," she said, words partly smothered by a fresh bout of aggrieved yowling from Lissah.

"It would be best if you kept her quiet," Guyime advised. "It's said a stone bear can hear a goat fart from ten miles away."

Her brow creased but she duly placed a hand on Lissah's head, the cat falling to instant silence. "I'll lead," Seeker said, starting off into the drifting fog. "Since there's something nearby likely to eat us."

Guyime lingered to wait for Orsena as Lorweth and Lexius followed Seeker. The Ultria's features betrayed a distracted air, one that switched to curiosity when she caught sight of the statue.

"I hadn't expected to find a cousin in stone," she said, a smile rising then falling from her lips, her head taking on an angle that Guyime knew signified an interjection from the inhabitant of the Conjurer's Blade. "It finds the carving crude and primitive," Orsena reported. Guyime saw how her hand went to the sword's hilt, twitched a little then shifted to her belt. "Apparently, it's rather keen on reshaping it."

"She," Guyime corrected. "Your demon bane is female now, so I'm told."

"Ah." Orsena frowned then let out a short laugh. "That actually makes a strange kind of sense."

Seeing her hand twitch again, Guyime added, "We've no time to waste on vandalising ancient art," he said.

Orsena winced, the sword at her side giving off a faint vibration. "She didn't like that," she said, forcing a smile.

"It doesn't matter what she likes." Guyime met Orsena's gaze squarely, putting a hard note of authority to his voice. "You are the wielder, not her. You have to remember that or she will make you her slave."

At first, Orsena bridled at his words, her bearing that of a noblewoman suffering an affront delivered by a commoner. Then her expression softened, the perfect planes of her faces shadowed by grim resolve. "As you've said before, your highness," she reminded him. "Many times."

"And will again, Ultria." Guyime stepped aside and bowed as he gestured to the rise ahead. "As often as it needs saying."

When Guyime had first traversed this path there had been a dozen Stone Bears marking the route. Now there were ten. What became of the other two would remain an unsolved mystery, though Seeker opined that the creatures they were intended to represent had toppled them in a fit of annoyance.

"Bears the world over are prideful," she said. "They don't like to be mocked."

Having never heard this woman utter a word that could be taken as a joke before, Guyime doubted she was doing so now. Although she continued to sense no danger throughout their trek along the statue-marked route, Guyime was relieved when the last granite monolith came into view near nightfall. It sat atop the steepest ridge they had yet climbed, the crest descending in a shallow arc to a broad plateau. A march of a dozen miles across this relatively flat expanse would bring them to Iron Shield Pass, the fortified cut through the mountains that marked the true border of the Northern Kingdom. Guyime disliked the notion of camping under the gaze of the Stone Bear, knowing Orsena's demon would pester her to rework it, but to press on in darkness invited disaster.

"This is the last of it," Lorweth said, dumping his supply of firewood into the circle of stones Lexius had gathered. "And what fine feast, may I ask, will you offer us tonight, my learned friend?"

"Porridge," Lexius said, extracting the sack of oats from his pack.

"Careful now." Lorweth gave a sour grunt as he slumped beside the fire, watching Lexius strike his flint to the kindling. "So much variety will surely confuse my palate, and it's a delicate thing, y'know."

"I once had a master who liked to feed me raw fish guts." Lexius offered Lorweth a bland smile before blowing gently on the burgeoning flames. "And make me eat them again when I spewed them up. So you will, I'm sure, forgive my dearth of sympathy, Master Druid."

Seeing Orsena engaged in a close inspection of the statue, Guyime moved to rest a hand on her shoulder. "Lessons?" she asked, glancing up at him.

"It befits one who carries a sword to learn how to use it."

Teaching her the basics of swordcraft had become a nightly ritual during the trek north. Guyime had offered to teach Lexius too but the scholar avowed little interest, saying, "When one possesses a blade capable of levelling a building with a single bolt of lightning, the nuances of thrust and parry seem somewhat redundant, my lord."

Orsena, by contrast, quickly became a keen student, absorbing a good deal of Guyime's tutelage with a swiftness he knew no mere human could match. Her creator had imbued her form with a grace and litheness the equal of any dancer whilst her muscles, if they could truly be called such, possessed a strength and stamina beyond any mortal warrior.

"Good," Guyime said, the wooden staves they used for practice clacking as they rebounded from one another, Orsena adopting a typically perfect sideways lunge to parry the slash he had directed at her shoulder. His approval dimmed, however, when, instead of pressing the slight advantage she had gained, she retreated a step to resume a defensive stance. He had noticed her lack of aggression before and found it worrisome. Soon they would be in the Northlands proper, a place where, if all he had heard of his former kingdom proved true, they were sure to encounter trouble.

"You don't win by retreating," he told her, jabbing a thrust at her belly which she easily evaded by means of an elegant pirouette.

"Why win when you can run?" she replied, fending off his follow-up strike at her legs. "Why kill when there's no need? I have been gifted with sufficient endurance to outlast most opponents. It's my hope to simply tire them into submission."

She spoke with a light tone but Guyime knew her words reflected a sincere inner conflict: she didn't want to kill. *No stomach for the fight, my liege,* Lakorath observed. *Won't do at all. Best drop her off a cliff, eh?*

"Real battle is never so simple," Guyime told her. "And I..." he struck without pause, the wooden blade coming within a hair's breadth of her throat before she batted it aside, "...have been restraining myself, thus far."

Seeing her mouth form a hard line and her body tense, Guyime adopted a defensive stance, awaiting her charge which would surely have been swiftly delivered if Seeker hadn't abruptly leapt to her feet.

"Arm yourselves!" the beast charmer snapped, hefting her bow and nocking an arrow to the string. Lissah crouched at her side, teeth bared in a snarling hiss as Seeker sank into a crouch, eyes unblinking as she scanned the misted gloom. The sky wasn't yet full dark but the lingering fog and gathering dusk made it impossible to make out anything beyond a dozen feet in each direction.

"Bears?" Guyime asked. Tossing his stave aside, he drew the Nameless Blade and moved to stand with his back to the fire, gesturing for the others to do the same.

"The scent is...unusual," Seeker replied. "But, yes. Bears." She paused and he saw a frown of self-reproach pass across her brow. "I should have sensed them before they got so close."

"Mountain bears are renowned for their cunning," Guyime said by way of mollification before glancing at Lorweth. "Master Druid." Guyime flicked a hand at the surrounding fog. "If you would be so kind."

Although Guyime knew Lorweth to be a man of many flaws, cowardly panic was not amongst them and the Mareth set himself to the task without demur. Raising his arms, he stepped away from the fire. The gale he crafted was weak by his standards, but deliberately so, intended only to dispel the mist. It thinned and receded in the face of the druid's winds, revealing gentle slopes to either side of their camp, the crests of which were lined with a long procession of bulky silhouettes. Guyime counted at least forty to one side and close on fifty to the other.

"Ah, bugger," Lorweth breathed. "Seems your tale was right, your worship, this is an army."

"It's the swords," Seeker said, nodding to Guyime's glowing blade. "This breed has magic in their blood and bones, and they don't like the stink of demons."

Charming, Lakorath drawled. *Can't say I'm fond of their stench either. Oh well, let's be about it, my liege. It's been decades since I tasted bear flesh.*

"Can you...?" Guyime asked Seeker, ignoring the demon's bloodlust.

The crease in Seeker's brow deepened as she stared hard at the shadowed figures above. "They sense me," she said, shaking her head, "hear me as other creatures do. But also they reject me. For the bond to work, it must be accepted willingly. I can do no more than birth fear in their hearts, which I suspect will only rouse their anger to a greater pitch."

"Lightning may work better," Guyime suggested, turning to Lexius.

"Don't!" Seeker warned as the scholar prepared to raise the Kraken's Tooth. "Use of magic will only enrage them."

"They sound fairly peeved as it is," Lorweth observed as a chorus of growls began to echo down the slopes. The rumbling tumult built steadily, forming a single ominous note of sufficient power and depth to add a tremble to the stone beneath Guyime's feet. He saw how the bears had begun to shift and bob, no doubt girding themselves for a charge.

Bear flesh for supper it is! Lakorath chimed in with hungry anticipation. *Mayhap when you're done this particular genus will be extinct. Another entry in the ledger of your notable achievements, my liege.*

Seeing a bear hurl itself down the slope, followed by a dozen more, Guyime gritted his teeth and took a firmer grip on the sword's handle. "Stay together," he told the others. "Lorweth, when they're close enough, raise a gale to hold them off. Lexius, burn as many as you can. Ultria, have a care for Seeker's person, if you would..."

As he spoke he turned towards Orsena, voice fading at the sight of her running from his side. *Craven bitch,* Lakorath sniffed. *Still, at least I won't have to listen to any more artistic babble.*

The demon's judgement, however, proved mistaken for Orsena quickly came to a halt at the base of the Stone Bear's statue. The Conjurer's Blade blazed a blinding shade of blue as she raised it, Guyime shielding his eyes from the glare that grew yet brighter when Orsena slashed at the Stone Bear's feet. The statue swayed and tilted at her initial blow, Guyime expecting it to topple onto the Ultria as she continued to wield the Conjurer's Blade. Orsena began to circle the Stone Bear, her sword moving with such swiftness its glow created a cage of light, one that soon merged into a unified ball of glowing blue energy.

A thunderclap of displaced air sent Guyime and the others reeling, a wall of grit and frost expanding out from the Stone Bear to leave them blinking. When Guyime's sight cleared, he found himself no longer regarding a statue.

Orsena backed away as her new creation took its first steps, tottering forward to sink to its forelegs, mighty head shaking in confusion. At first Guyime thought it much the same as the statues the doomed shade of Temesia Alvenisci had brought to life in her last desperate attempts to destroy the Exultia caste of Atheria. However, as the bear huffed and shuffled forward, he saw that its pelt was fur rather than stone. Also its eyes possessed a definite sense of awareness as it scanned its surroundings, narrowing in suspicion at the small humans clustered nearby, then widening in recognition at the bears dotting the surrounding slopes.

They had all come to a sudden halt, their charge abandoned, each one crouched in what Guyime felt to be a subservient huddle. The chorus of growls had faded and the bears kept their snouts lowered and eyes averted. This cowed attitude abruptly became panicked distress when the newly animated statue raised itself up onto its hind legs and let out a roar.

The sound, a harsh, grating wall of fury, pealed out to echo amongst the mountains with the force of a storm, sending the bears into instant flight. By the time the roar ended they had vanished from the slopes.

The Stone Bear grunted as it dropped onto all fours, shared a short but, Guyime felt, meaningful glance with Orsena, then loped away. It scattered stone and dust in its wake before cresting the southerly slope and disappearing from view.

"She's not sure how long he'll live," Orsena said. She briefly twirled the Conjurer's Blade before slipping it into her scabbard. "Perhaps only a century or two. Now," she briskly clapped her hands together and returned to the campfire, "I believe porridge is on the menu."

Chapter Two

Iron Shield Pass

When Guyime had last traversed Iron Shield pass his face had been hidden beneath an unkempt beard and a ragged hood lest the soldiers stationed there recognise the man they had called king only weeks before. It had been a heavily garrisoned and well-maintained fortress then, the twin towers flanking the narrow cut through the mountains scrubbed clean and crowned by huge banners bearing the sigil of House Mathille. Eyeing the grey, soot-streaked walls now, Guyime doubted they had felt the touch of a scrubbing brush for the better part of a decade. Also, the sole banner was a small thing of white and blue, its sigil impossible to make out from this distance. As they drew nearer he counted only a dozen sentries on the towers and the same number on the barrier wall below, pole-axes tilted to the signature angle of bored or slovenly soldiery.

A disgraceful display, my liege, Lakorath agreed, sensing Guyime's disapproval. *Force one in ten to choose lots to face the noose and flog the rest. Always used to work a treat for discipline, as I recall.*

The impression of disorder was further enhanced by the contingent that greeted them at the fortress gate. It stood open as was the norm during daylight, allowing for the passage of traveller and merchant which were sparse at this time of year but not unknown. However, any resemblance to the stern and scrupulous soldiers Guyime had once set to guard this portal was singularly absent from the gang of unshaven, ill-kempt villains who glowered at the approaching party.

"State your business," the sergeant stated in gruff annoyance, he and his men moving to bar their path. One look at this man's sallow, stubbled features and weary gaze was enough for Guyime to conclude he had achieved his rank by dint of size alone. There was also a hollow cast to his eyes and those of his soldiers, the kind Guyime was accustomed to seeing on the faces of those who have recently survived arduous battle. But what battle could arise here?

"Trade, good captain," Lorweth told the sergeant. The druid had a gift for engaging with even the most truculent souls, usually via a combination of flattery and judicious lies. Consequently, and fearing his own temper, Guyime was content to leave the inevitable negotiation in Lorweth's hands.

"Trade my arse," the sergeant responded, sunken eyes tracking from Lorweth to his companions. "Gang of cutthroats come north for the wars, more like." He paused to spit, though Guyime felt there to be an air of routine to his apparent anger. "May the Ravager's black soul claim the lot of you."

It appears we have a worthy candidate for impalement, Lakorath said, voice imbued with a certain happy nostalgia. *I always did like the way they squirmed when the pike skewered them from arsehole to gizzard. You remember that one fellow who was still begging as the spearpoint came out of his mouth…*

"Just honest travellers come north in search of goods to purchase, captain," Lorweth assured the sergeant, giving a meaningful pat to his purse. It was filled with silver drawn from Orsena's family vaults, one of several they carried for such occasions. "Nor will we shirk our payment of all necessary tolls."

The sergeant's scowl shifted to a brief frown of calculation. Although patently a dullard, Guyime had noted before how men such as this were remarkably swift when it came to gauging the correct amount for a bribe.

"What coinage do you bear?" he grunted at Lorweth.

"Atherian talents." Lorweth extracted one of the coins from the purse. It flickered as the druid tossed it into the sergeant's open palm, a perfectly round and clearly embossed circle of silver which contrasted with crudely minted local coinage. The gleam in the sergeant's eye matched that of the coin, though Guyime could tell his greed wasn't yet satiated.

"One won't suffice," he said. "Since you're bearing weapons, the law demands three. Can't just let you southland villains wander through this gate without proper recompense for all the havoc you'll wreak."

Grasping dolt, Lakorath sneered. *Perhaps you should flay him as you impale him, my liege…*

Guyime's regal pride was a mostly dormant thing, but he felt a pricking to it at the sergeant's naked avarice. Still, he was long practised in resisting Lakorath's ugly urgings. Orsena, judging by the way her hand tensed on the hilt of the Conjurer's Blade, was having considerably more difficulty combating her own demonic companion.

"She doesn't like rudeness," she murmured when Guyime placed a restraining hand on her arm. "Neither do I, in point of fact."

Deciding it was time to conclude this matter, Guyime took a step forward, to the alarm of the sergeant and his men. "Careful," the sergeant warned as the pole-axes descended to point their blades at Guyime's chest.

"Four silver talents," he said, extracting his own purse from the goat-skin jerkin he wore. "Three for passage, one for information."

For men such as this greed would always carry more weight than caution. Accordingly, the sergeant nudged his guards to lower their weapons, eyes flicking to Guyime but mostly captured by the sight of the three additional talents he extracted from his purse. "What," a small tongue, discoloured by ale and pipe smoke, emerged to lick the sergeant's lips, "information?"

"I believe a girl passed through here not long ago," Guyime said, nodding at Seeker. "A girl who looked much like her."

Seeker had been wearing a woollen scarf over her nose and mouth to ward against the chill, and removed it now to reveal her face in full. Guyime expected either blank ignorance or more bargaining from the sergeant, an irritating exchange that inevitably saw him handing over another talent or two. Any more than that and he might find himself succumbing to Lakorath's tempting suggestions. So it was a stark surprise when the sergeant's face abruptly took on far paler shade as his eyes slid over Seeker's features. More surprising still was the way in which he and his guards, now also considerably less flush of pallor, shifted from their path.

"One silver," the sergeant muttered, consigning Lorweth's tossed coin to his pocket. He and the other soldiers retreated to press themselves against the walls of the gatehouse, heads lowered in a manner that put Guyime in mind of the humbled bears back in the mountains. "Which you've paid." The sergeant jerked his head at the open cart-rutted track leading into the gloomy narrows of the pass. "Now piss off."

Seeker exchanged a short but weighty glance with Guyime before approaching the sergeant, standing close and staring hard into his downcast features. "You will look at me," she told him in her laboured but clear north-tongue.

It took a prolonged interval of fidgeted coughing before the sergeant consented to meet her gaze, a task performed with the air of a man seeing no option but to risk all by reaching into a snake pit. "Please," he pleaded in a whisper. "Don't."

"Don't do what?" Seeker enquired. She moved closer still, putting her face within an inch of the quailing soldier. "Do what she did? She had my face, did she not? Only younger?"

The sergeant's lips were set in a quivering but firmly closed line, though he did consent to nod.

"Did she carry a weapon, a dagger?" Seeker asked, drawing another nod and, Guyime saw, a burgeoning of tears in the man's eyes.

"Please," he pleaded again. "I can't…"

"What happened when she came here?" Seeker cut in, her face now so close to his that it seemed they were about to share a kiss. "What did she do to you?"

"She…" the discoloured tongue darted forth once more, twisting as it made passage over dry, trembling lips. "She just seemed a girl at first. We asked for our due but she had no coin, so…the lads said she could pay another way."

"And she didn't like that," Seeker said. "Did she?"

A wide-eyed, frantic shake of his head, the sergeant's next words emerging in a sob, "She drew that dagger, but not to fight. Instead, the blade glowed red, so bright it blinded us... and it made us dream. All of us, all at once. We all fell asleep and...those dreams."

The soldier to the sergeant's left began to weep then, hugging himself as he slid slowly down the wall. The others were only marginally less distressed, all shivering in mingled terror and misery.

"When we woke she was gone," the sergeant said. "'Cept not all of us woke. A few couldn't be roused no matter what we tried. It was like they were trapped in sleep, trapped in those dreams." His hand were twisting together now, fingers tracing over each other as if trying to wash them clean. "There was nothing else to be done. A mercy, it was."

He fell silent, staring at Seeker in mingled terror and expectation, a man unable to escape a returned nightmare. Guyime saw a small pulse of shame pass across the beast charmer's brow before she stepped back from the man, turning and striding into the pass without another word.

"This outpost is a disgrace," Guyime informed the still-unmoving sergeant as the others followed Seeker through the gate. "Either do the duty you've been given or take yourselves off somewhere."

The sergeant stared at him, apparently too terrorised to speak. Then, as Guyime turned away, he blurted out, "And the dreams? They come back, y'see? Every night."

"Drink more," Guyime advised, tossing another silver talent over his shoulder. "Or give yourself the mercy you gave your men."

"What has it made of her?" Seeker's voice was soft, the bowl of stew sitting untouched on the table before her. Around them, the sounds and sights of a surprisingly cheerful inn created an intrusive contrast to Seeker's mood. The place lay only a few miles north of Iron Shield pass, a substantial three-storey building situated alongside a crossroads busy with caravans. Guyime noted that most of the laden carts were proceeding either north or west, with few heading south and none heading east. Always, a crossroads proved a reliable gauge of where trouble could be found in any realm.

"Ekiri's grandfather used to say her soul had been woven by the Four Spirits from a thread of pure kindness," Seeker went on, gaze distant and brow troubled. "So sweet was she I worried the world would prove too a harsh a place for her. Now she crafts nightmares to torment men to madness and murder."

"Clearly the Crystal Dagger is powerful," Guyime said. "But we learned that in Atheria."

"The thing within it has claimed her." Seeker's eyes rose to meet his, steady and demanding. "Hasn't it?"

"We don't know that, not with certainty. I have carried this thing on my back for longer than I care to remember, and it has never mastered me. The same may be true of her."

"Then what is she doing? What is her goal?"

"More questions we can't answer until we find her." Guyime reached out to touch a hand to the guard on Seeker's wrist, the leather rough and worn for she had loosed many arrows in her life. "And find her we will. As I swore to you we would."

"You did." The demand in her eyes dimmed a little, but not completely. "As you swore to bring the Seven Swords together.

We do not know all we need to, that is true. But we do know that you can only claim your prize through her. Ekiri is the key." Seeker angled her head, tone lowering to voice a sincerely spoken promise. "Know this, Pilgrim: I will abide no harm to my daughter. You can have your swords, I don't care. But should the choice come between your purpose and securing her life, it will be no choice."

They held each other's gaze for a time, in understanding if not concordance, until the others returned to the table. Lorweth's fists clutched flagons of ale whilst Lexius brought more helpings of stew. Orsena had spent a time delighting the few children in the inn by allowing them to pet Lissah. Besides Seeker, the Ultria was the only other member of their party whose touch the caracal would willingly tolerate and the sight of so exotic a beast in the arms of so comely a woman inevitably served to garner interest, and loosen tongues.

"It's much as we heard on the road," Orsena said, extending an arm to enable Lissah to make passage from her shoulder to her mistress's lap. "Wars, rebellions, famine and strife abound." The Ultria spoke in flawless north-tongue coloured by a slight noble accent. Like many of her acquired skills, the learning of unfamiliar speech was a task she performed with effortless speed. The others all spoke the language of Guyime's homeland with varying degrees of skill, Lorweth and Orsena being the most fluent. Lexius' version was surprisingly harsh and heavily accented, albeit spoken with the precision of a learned man. Seeker was the least accomplished, but her sojourns through the southern ports of the Five Seas had made her conversant in languages common to trade.

"Mostly in the east, I take it?" Guyime asked.

"So they say, your worship," Lorweth confirmed. "There's a fellah who calls himself king in the west claims overlordship of what was the Great Northern Kingdom, but not all see fit to bow or pay the necessary tributes. Apparently, there's been talk of a grand campaign to unify his realm for years, but nothing ever seems to come of it."

Guyime reached into his pack for the Cartographer's map, shifting tankards and bowls to unfurl it on the table. "Strange happenings?" He scanned the mostly inert lines on the chart as he spoke. "Sudden calamities?"

"There's talk of plague in the east," Orsena replied. "As well as war. This is a troubled land indeed, your highness."

She spoke softly but the honorific still drew a warning glance from him. Just one evening in this inn and he had heard the name 'Ravager' expressed as a curse a dozen times or more.

"There was a curious tale or two," Lorweth added. "But little beyond the normal rumours of strangeness you hear on the road. 'Cepting maybe what that donkey-drover told me about a cursed castle."

For weeks the lines on the Cartographer's map had consented only to keep winding north through the mountains before taking on an indistinct dormancy when they neared Iron Shield pass. Now, however, mention of a cursed castle brought them to life. The faded swirls darkened and shifted, coalescing around the spot Guyime judged to represent their current locale.

"What castle?" he said, eyes still locked on the chart.

"Just an unlikely tale about a young knight from the western duchies," Lorweth said. "The drover happened upon him and his entourage some miles north. Supposedly, this noble lad will secure the hand of his lady love if he manages to hold some pile of stones for a year. Been trying to hire soldiers for the garrison but there's few takers. Not an easy thing persuading folk to journey into plague-ridden lands. Also, by all accounts the place has an evil reputation."

As the druid spoke, the lines on the map formed into familiar tendrils that, Guyime knew, signified the identification of a new destination. He felt scant surprise when they coalesced into overlapping lines and began to track east.

"The name of this pile of stones?" he asked.

"Blackfold Keep, the drover said, or something similar."

"No." Guyime watched the swirling tendrils form a single line that proceeded to snake through hills and forests before halting to blossom into an ugly black spot. As it did so a pictogram appeared beside it, one that signified a lake. "Blackfyre Keep," he murmured.

"You know it?" Orsena asked.

"By repute only," Guyime said. "And the druid has it right: it's an ill-omened place."

Memories swirled as he continued to regard the unsightly blot on the map, summoning forth the handsome face of Sir Lorent Athil, the only one of his Twelve most stalwart companions to survive Saint Maree's Field.

"An old comrade of mine was greatly fascinated with the castle's story," Guyime went on. "And would sometimes regale us with it when the hour grew long at the campfire. Sir Lorent had no castle of his own, you see, it had been taken from his family generations before. So he dreamed of claiming another." Guyime paused, deciding not to include the fact that Sir Lorent had intended that fierce Lady Ihlene should be at his side when he claimed his keep. Speaking of their love felt like a betrayal, perhaps because they had never spoken of it, not even to each other.

"I think the notion of cleansing a supposedly cursed holdfast appealed to his chivalrous nature," he continued. "For he was, in truth, the only knight I ever met to be worthy of being called such. The tale of the keep's cursing is an old one, dating back to the Barons' War a century before my time. The king crushed a rebellion led by traitorous nobles of the eastern baronies. Once they had all been beheaded in accordance with law and custom, he seized their lands and castles to be parcelled out as rewards to his loyal knights. One of the unfortunate barons, however, had a son who took to the hills with a faithful band of followers. His name was Orwin Blackfyre, and he swore the bloodiest vengeance on any western lord the king sent to occupy his father's castle. It proved no idle boast.

"Over the course of a dozen years Orwin, through guile and, some say, the dark magics of the eastern hill-folk, slew every soul who dared to take up residence in Blackfyre Keep. Not just the lords, but their retainers and servants too. In time, no western knight could be prevailed upon to hold it, and Orwin grew bold enough to return and proclaim himself Baron Blackfyre. But there was no triumph for Orwin, for in his pursuit of vengeance he had grown monstrous, vile of temper and unjust in his rule. It's said the hill witch who had lent her magic to his rebellion turned against him, cursing him and all who followed him. Since they were so keen on holding the castle, she cursed them to hold it forever, even beyond death. So the story goes that the keep, long abandoned, remains home to Lord Orwin and his phantom band of rebels who have never lost their lust for blood."

Lorweth's dispirited sigh scattered froth from his ale as he brought the tankard to his lips. "Couldn't have been a nice pleasant, sunlit island in the balmier portions of the Third Sea, could it?" he muttered.

"No, Master Druid," Guyime said, furling the map. "It couldn't. Where exactly do we find this ardent knight? I've a sense that venturing into the eastern reaches without benefit of armed company will not be wise, even for us."

Chapter Three

The Squire and the Knight

The knight's squire was a slab of a man, standing taller than Guyime by an inch or more with an intimidating breadth of bone and muscle to match. At first glance Guyime had assumed the squire to be north of his thirtieth year, but seeing his features at closer remove, realised he must be nearer to twenty. His face was all stark lines lacking any fat and a strong jaw and nose that most would term more brutish than handsome. However, his youth did not make him a fool, Guyime seeing equal parts shrewd appraisal and suspicion as the squire surveyed the five strange persons gathered before the cart where he had perched himself.

They had arrived at this muddy cluster of hovels in late morning, finding this fellow hallooing passersby from atop his cart in a vain attempt to entice them to join his master's mission. A poorly inscribed plank-wood sign proclaimed 'Soldiers - Ten Shellings a week. Archers - twenty.' In Guyime's day a man-at-arms would count himself wealthy if he earned a shelling a month, but such were the vagaries of commerce. Judging by the wide berth passersby afforded him, along with occasional ribald insults, even these apparently generous wages hadn't sufficed to draw any recruits to the Squire's banner. Yet, when presented with five willing volunteers, the fellow proved reluctant.

"Sea-folk is it?" he asked, having allowed a long interval to pass following Lorweth's typically florid introduction. 'Sea-folk' was the universal and somewhat apt northern term for any foreigner who hailed from south of the mountains where the Five Seas dominated all life and trade. "Not you, though," the squire added, eyes narrowing as he took a closer look at Lorweth. His gaze grew yet more suspicious upon shifting to Guyime. "Or you, I'd guess. The kiss of the sun bronzes the skin but doesn't hide your origins. What duchy do you hail from?"

Shrewd he may have been but this question bespoke a distinct lack of experience in hiring mercenaries. "A man's past is his own," Guyime told him. "I have a sword and the skills to use it. My associates are equally worthy of pay for dangerous work." He nodded to his companions before giving a pointed glance to the mostly bare lane of rutted mud. "Whilst you appear to be in dire want of folk such as us. Nothing else should concern you at this juncture."

The squire's caution apparently didn't extend to his temper, for his heavy features took on an angry flush. "I'll take no lectures on how to conduct my business from you…"

"If I may, good sir," Lorweth broke in, bowing low as he placed himself between Guyime and the squire. "You'll have to forgive our captain. So many battles will coarsen a man's manners. Such has it ever been for the Iron Dogs." He straightened, taking on an air of prideful expectation.

"Iron Dogs?" the squire asked, squinting.

"Why, yes." Lorweth laughed in apparent surprise. "The very hounds of the red sands themselves." He paused again, allowing the squire's bemusement to continue. "The victors of the Execration?" Lorweth added, seemingly baffled by the man's ignorance. "Veterans of a hundred skirmishes in the feuds of Carthula and saviours of Atheria. Sir," Lorweth stepped back, arms spread to encompass their band, "I tell you no lie. These are truly the Iron Dogs and no other."

"Never heard of you." The squire spoke gruffly but his temper had cooled. "They bear weapons," he noted, jerking his head at Guyime and the others before looking closer at Lorweth. "But you've got nothing more than a knife. What makes you worth hiring, besides your flowery tongue?"

Lorweth raised an eyebrow at Guyime and, receiving a nod, offered the squire a broad smile. "I'd guess you've been standing there a while," he said. "Perhaps you would welcome a cooling breeze."

The wind he conjured was far too strong to be termed a breeze, raising flecks of mud from the road that created a brown whirlwind around the squire's cart before Lorweth let it fade. It was hardly his most spectacular display but it did serve to impress the squire, although a good deal of caution lingered on his face as he afforded the druid a long look of appraisal.

"Can't offer more than twenty-five shellings a week," he said. "Even for a mage."

"Thirty," Guyime stated. "And the same for the rest of us." He gave a thin smile. "The Iron Dogs are not beggars."

Had he not stood next to the squire, Guyime felt Sir Anselm Challice would have made a far more impressive figure. As it was, this tall young man with his cascade of dark silken hair and an undeniably handsome face appeared little more than a callow youth as he stood in his tent pondering the words of his hulking bondsman.

"They claim to be famous warrior band from the seas, my lord," he said. "Can't speak to the truth of that but the Mareth's a mage and may prove useful. Not sure his worth amounts to thirty a week, mind."

"Thirty eh?" Sir Anselm mused, frowning as he looked Lorweth over before surveying the rest of the recently named Iron Dogs. Like many a young man, his gaze lingered on Orsena, but not so much as was usual, and most of his attention fell on Guyime.

"Would I be wrong in marking you as leader of this band, sir?" he enquired.

"No," Guyime said simply, watching Anselm's focus track to the sword handle jutting above his shoulder. The pommel, handle and hilt were wrapped in leather and fur which served to conceal much of its finery. However, the metal that showed through was untarnished and bare of any scratches. To the uneducated eye it would appear a weapon of considerable worth and very much at odds with the grizzled appearance of the man who carried it.

"That's an unfamiliar pattern," Anselm observed, extending a hand. "May I see it?"

"Our captain has religious convictions that forbid such things," Lorweth interjected quickly, adding a servile, "my lord," for good measure.

"Ah," Anselm said. He pursed his lips in a manner that told Guyime that this man, like his squire, was no fool, even if he had embarked upon a fool's mission. "And what name do you go by, captain?"

"Just Captain will do," Guyime told him.

"As you wish." A frown appeared on the knight's brow then, his head tilting to an inquisitive angle. "Curious accent you have, Captain. I'd place it in the mid-realm duchies, but it has a lilt to it I've not heard since my grandfather passed."

Guyime stared back at Anselm for a time, searching his face for some inkling of possibly dangerous knowledge. *And thus the seed of suspicion is sown, my liege,* Lakorath murmured. *One that will surely grow. Best slit his throat when an opportune moment, arises, eh?*

"I was told you needed fighters for a journey into the eastern baronies," Guyime said. "The price is thirty shellings each per week for myself and my dogs. This price is not to be bargained over. I will tolerate no further questioning of myself or my company. You pay us to march and fight under your banner, that is all. Our loyalty ends when the pay ends. This is the code of those who follow the path of the hired blade. If you can't meet these terms, we'll be on our way."

He started towards the tent flap and ducked to pull it aside, then paused at the knight's command. "Stop!" Anselm's voice possessed the kind of authoritative snap that only came from those born to importance. Position in the court of King Guyime, known the world over as the Ravager, had been earned and never inherited. Therefore, such a tone would once have provoked Guyime to spend a short interval beating some respect into this privileged whelp. The Captain of the Iron Dogs, however, merely straightened and raised an eyebrow.

"Thirty shellings apiece it is," Anselm said, inclining his head, much to the consternation of his squire.

"My lord…" he began, voice low as he moved to the knight's side.

"Hector me not, Galvin," Anselm told him, waving a hand in dismissal. "We've tarried in this mud-trap long enough. Adding our new recruits to the household men-at-arms brings our strength to fifty all told."

"Forty-nine, my lord," Galvin corrected. "Delvis died of the flux yesterday."

"Oh yes." Anselm frowned for a fractional moment before a brisk smile came to his lips. "No matter, I've known blind cripples who made better archers. Muster the company, Galvin. I wish to be well on the road by nightfall."

"And the plague, my lord? We hear more talk of it every passing day." Galvin's features had the look of a man caging words he knew his master didn't want to hear. From the way he looked at the knight, Guyime could tell that this man's loyalty went far beyond ingrained servility.

"Father Lothare's blessing will repel the ill-humours, I'm sure. By all accounts that man's prayers can turn aside a tempest. So a little sickness is hardly likely to trouble him."

The last priest of the Risen Church Guyime had encountered called himself Book and, at the end of a long and difficult journey, had revealed himself to be a duplicitous murderer. He had died screaming whilst a demon warlord pretending godhood burned scripture into his bones for idle amusement.

Guyime felt Book's end had been overly merciful, but then, he tended to think much the same of all clerics in service to this particular church. They came in disparate shapes and sizes, afflicted with varying degrees of devotion or hypocrisy, but it had been many a year since he met one he hadn't wanted to kill. Father Lothare, grey-robed and grey-bearded but stoutly built with a harsh yet compelling voice, proved no exception. However, the absence of cynical deceit from Lothare's gaze did at least set him apart from the treacherous fanatic who shared Guyime's pilgrimage through the Execration.

An unlucky fall one dark night, perhaps? Lakorath suggested as Guyime watched the priest bless the holy mission of Sir Anselm Challice and his brave company. *The rest of these grovellers will surely take a dim view of openly murdering their cleric.*

Sir Anselm's household men-at-arms knelt in a field alongside the carts stacked high with furled tents and supplies whilst Father Lothare gently swung a brass aspergil over their bowed heads. He canted his blessing as he worked the chain to swing the device which resembled a ball affixed to a narrow cylinder, scattering water onto the assembled soldiery.

"May the First Risen bless our steps," Lothare repeated in his strident voice. "May His Grace guide our hand. May the First Risen bless our steps…"

"What's in that thing?" Seeker asked, brow furrowed in bemusement. As foreign heathens, they had been spared the ceremony and stood alongside the carts watching with disparate levels of interest. Seeker and Lorweth displayed an aversion to the whole spectacle, the druid positioning himself atop a cart bed in apparent slumber whilst Seeker prowled the grassy verge of the road with Lissah at her side.

"The blood of the First Risen," Guyime replied, seeing how several soldiers flinched as the droplets found their skin.

Orsena's frown deepened. "It doesn't look like blood."

"It's water when it's in the holy aspergil," Guyime explained. "It becomes blood when he casts it forth amidst the words of his blessing, only appearing to remain water."

Orsena's brows took on an amused, disdainful arch. "That makes no modicum of sense whatsoever."

"Actually," Lexius put in, "it does, when you consider the power of faith."

"How so?"

"Faith carries power, but such power derives from its detachment from reason. A true believer in the Risen Church will feel no doubt that they have felt the touch of the very blood of the First Risen, whilst those weak in their faith will feel and see only water."

"So," Orsena's mouth quirked in restrained mirth, "it's blood because they want it to be."

"Not want," Guyime said, still watching the priest with steady eyes. "Need. They need it to be blood, otherwise it's all just nonsense and they've been grovelling to shadows their entire lives."

An unfortunate accident, Lakorath reminded him. A paradoxical feature of their unnatural bonding was that, when it came to the subject of priests, it was usually the demon's role to advocate caution. *And best not done until a few days have elapsed.*

"Well then, my new exotic friends." Sir Anselm's bearing was all cheery eagerness as he trotted his horse towards them when the blessing was done. "To the road. I've a yen to scout the ground ahead, be so kind as to have a care for the carts."

"It would be better, my lord," Guyime said, tone flat with forced patience, "if you left the scouting to myself and my companion." He nodded to where Seeker stood on the verge. "There's not a scent nor a track beyond her senses."

"My thanks, Captain." Anselm's smile remained undimmed as he inclined his head at Guyime. "But this is not my first foray into danger. Three wars have I fought and hunted more beasts than I can count."

With that, he laughed, wheeled his impressive black destrier about and rode off in a cloud of raised sod.

"Young, foolish and arrogant," Orsena said, falling in alongside Guyime as the carters snapped their reins and sent the oxen into motion. "And yet he commands so many."

They walked at a remove of a dozen paces on either side of the carts which followed the main body of men-at-arms marching in tidy order along the eastward road. Besides Anselm, Galvin was the only other mounted member of the company and he stayed with the men. Guyime could tell their discipline resulted from the way the squire constantly scanned their ranks, gaze sharp with near predatory anticipation. Sir Anselm might have the rank but Guyime knew whose voice these men answered to.

"Men and women are set high by dint of birth here," Guyime told her. "A concept I would have thought familiar to you, Ultria."

Orsena frowned in the faintly amused manner that indicated a refusal to rise to one of his occasional taunts. "The Exultia breed so infrequently that such notions are, in fact, somewhat alien in Atheria," she said. "And, whilst true power rests in the hands of but one caste, we are not so foolish as to risk dangers best left to others. Except, of course, in my case."

She fixed Guyime with a disconcertingly dazzling smile. "My person being so very exceptional."

Father Lothare appeared at their campfire that night, striding unheralded out of the gloom to perch himself between Seeker and Lorweth. "That smells good," he said by way of introduction, nodding to the cook-pot suspended over the fire. "May I prevail upon your charity, brothers and sisters?" He held out an empty bowl to Lexius as the scholar tended to the mutton stew steaming in the pot.

They had established their camp a short distance from the rest of the company, Guyime opting to take up position on a low rise rather than amongst the carts. Only a few miles of eastward marching and the road had worsened considerably, degenerating into a pale brown track across mostly uncultivated fields. Guyime recalled the aggravating flatness of the land from the campaigns he once waged here. Such featureless ground negated the chances of ambush but also ensured his enemies could easily mark his approach from far away. Bringing the region to heel had required months of forced marches that cost him more soldiers than actual battle.

"As long as you're not minded to pray over it first," Guyime said. It was a calculated barb, intended to provoke outrage and gauge the man's devotion. In both respects it failed, for Lothare merely grunted a laugh as Lexius returned his bowl, now brimming with stew.

"Done my praying for the night, Captain," the priest said, smiling thanks at Lexius.

"Warded off the ill-humours, have you?" Guyime put a deliberately sour edge to his voice. "Sir Anselm seems to be labouring under the delusion that prayer alone will shield us from plague."

Once again the priest ignored the bait, merely taking an experimental bite of stew and affording Lexius a nod of appreciation. "You cook well for a scholar, sir," he said. "Though I believe the correct term is 'Lexius', is it not?"

"Both my name and my role," Lexius replied. "You've a keen eye, Father."

"More the ear than the eye. There's a clear Carthulan lilt to your voice, but it's too coarse to be anything but the product of the slave pens." He took another mouthful of stew before adding, "No offence."

"You've been to Carthula?" Guyime asked.

"I have. In my youth I took pilgrimage to the homeland of the First Risen, a sojourn that carried me all over the Five Seas. So, I know that this fine lady," Lothare nodded at Orsena, "despite her colouring and the absence of a mask, is a high caste denizen of the fine city of Atheria. That scowling druid is a Mareth, though his pallor and clothing indicate a widely travelled man. The huntress hails from one of the Beast Charmer clans south of the Second Sea and her cat is only found in the deserts around Salish. Then there's you, Captain."

The priest's frown deepened as he chewed mutton and considered Guyime's person. "You, I must confess, are a good deal more difficult to place." The calculation in his gaze and lack of concern at any annoyance it might cause stirred a roiling in Guyime's gut and put an itch to his sword hand.

An unfortunate accident, my liege, Lakorath cautioned.

"Do they really ward off plague?" Orsena asked the priest, interrupting his scrutiny. "Your prayers, I mean to say."

"Prayers are of the soul, my lady, whilst plague is very much of the body. However, the Arisen do occasionally see fit to succour the faithful in times of privation or sickness."

"So, the more faithful they are the more the chance of… divine intervention?" Orsena's quizzical expression contained a patent taunt, one that Guyime felt had found a mark where his hadn't.

"True devotion is found only in the depths of the soul," Father Lothare replied, a faintly defensive note creeping into his voice. "Its truth is ultimately only for the Arisen to know, but…" The priest trailed off, gaze straying to Sir Anselm's tent. The banner of the knight's house fluttered from a standard sprouting from the tent, a spread winged eagle clutching a cup. "There are other forms of devotion, and other forms of faith."

"It's true then?" Guyime asked. "He mounted this entire enterprise to win the love of a woman?"

"If you had ever glimpsed the person of Lady Elsinora of Ellgren, you might understand why." Lothare's features shaded in reflective sorrow as he returned his attention to his meal. "To love fiercely and not be loved in return is a more terrible curse than anything a demon could conjure."

I wouldn't be too sure of that, Lakorath chimed in.

"This mission was the lady's idea," Guyime said. "A means to rid herself of an unwanted suitor."

"She could have just said no," Orsena remarked.

"She did, my lady," Lothare assured her. "Many times. But besotted youths are ever the deafest of creatures. In truth, I believe this quest was her mother's idea. Sir Anselm would make a fine catch for many ladies, but Elsinora has always been destined for royal favour."

"Then it will make no difference if he holds the keep for a year," Guyime concluded. "The lady's family would never allow a marriage in any case. This is a hopeless enterprise. Which begs the question of why, then, are you here, Father? You don't strike me as a foolish man."

Lothare chewed his stew for a time, a preoccupied cast to his brow. "My pilgrimage took me to many lands," he said. "I saw many things, many dark things. I learned that evil lurks in the shadows of this world and it is my role, as a priest in service to a church that brings light to the darkness, to banish evil. If the stories are true, Blackfyre Keep is a place beset by the worst of evils, so that is where I shall go."

He turned to Guyime with an affable smile. "Which also begs the question, why are you here, Captain?"

"Pay and the prospect of slaughter," Guyime said, enjoying the fact that his words finally succeeded in putting a small crease of disapproval in the cleric's brow. "What else does a hired blade delight in?"

Chapter Four

The Sickened Lands

The weather grew progressively worse the further east they marched, the road transforming from a dry scrape across the earth to a muddy furrow as repeated lashings of chill rain fell from a perpetually overcast sky. Although it was late in the season, Guyime would have expected to find many crops awaiting harvest. However, it was clear that the puddle-dotted fields they passed hadn't felt the plough's blade for weeks. Also, every farmstead and cottage they encountered proved empty and scoured of all but the meanest possessions.

Nothing we haven't seen before, my liege, Lakorath observed as the company made its way through a collection of abandoned hovels. *Remember the year of the Grey Flux on the shore of the Fourth Sea? The air was thick with the with perfume of sickness and suffering. The bodies piled so high it seemed as if the locals were trying to build a mountain of corpses.*

"I remember," Guyime said, his eyes slipping towards Father Lothare striding along as he engaged Lexius in a discussion of Carthulan theology. "They had priests of their own who told them the dead should be collected together so that the gods could contain sickness in one place. The rats grew fat and plentiful and the stink was perhaps the worst I've ever known. And the flux raged unchecked until the rains finally came and it faded."

Quite so, Lakorath agreed with a wistful sigh before continuing in a marginally more serious tone. *Curious then that I sense no sickness here. Human pestilence is a sweet scent for my kind, and I can detect not the slightest whiff. There's a lingering stench of fear, certainly. But whatever caused these people to flee, it wasn't plague.*

Seeing Seeker pause and sink into a familiar crouch, Guyime moved to her side. The beast charmer played her hand over a patch of mud, softened by the rain but marked as disturbed ground by the way it contrasted with the sparse grass that surrounded it. Lissah had retreated a good distance, pacing to and fro whilst her tail curled in a signature display of distress.

"A grave?" Guyime asked as Seeker leaned closer to the ground, nostrils flaring.

"It was," she confirmed. "Now it's empty."

"No marker." He scanned the village, finding no sign of a graveyard, which wasn't unusual for a settlement of this size. Folk from smaller villages would usually take their dead to the nearest chapel for funeral rites. Yet, before they fled, the inhabitants of this place had seen fit to consign a body to the earth without benefit of clergy or the customary mound of stones placed at the grave's head by mourners. Also, someone had later decided to disinter the grave's occupant.

"Scavengers?" he suggested. "Wild dogs will drag a corpse from the ground. Wolves too if they're hungry enough."

Seeker shook her head, standing to scan the surrounding country before exchanging a brief, wordless glance with Lissah. Guyime sensed a certain reluctance in the way the caracal bared her fangs before bounding off, making for the stone wall marking the village's northern boundary. Guyime followed as Seeker set off in pursuit at a steady run. Vaulting the wall, they traversed the unkempt field beyond, Guyime noting the un-reaped turnips rotting in the soil before seeing Lissah had come to a halt twenty paces off. She described a rapid circle as she waited for Seeker, displaying an even greater level of distress. The source was not hard to identify.

The body lay face down, flesh bleached white. His garb was mean but mostly intact, sodden from the rains but Guyime made out the dark stains that discoloured the coarse fabric. Coming closer, he judged the corpse as male, old too given the deep creases around his one visible eye, although death had a habit of accentuating such things. His few teeth were yellow beads revealed by lips set in a rictus snarl, jaw gaping wide and mouth half-filled with mud. It appeared as if he had been frozen in the act of trying to eat the earth.

"Best not get too close," Guyime advised Seeker as she went to her haunches beside the body. "Plague lingers in the bones even after death."

"There's no sickness here," she replied, eyes keen as she surveyed the corpse from head to toe.

As I said, Lakorath added. *I'd say this fellow's heart gave out some days ago. And look at his flesh. Nary a bite from dog or crow. In fact, it's been a day or two since I heard a bird call.*

The drum of hooves on damp ground drew Guyime's eyes to the sight of Sir Anselm and Galvin riding towards them across the field.

"Finally found ourselves a peasant, have we?" the knight asked, reining in his destrier to afford the body a brief glance of appraisal. "Doesn't appear he'll be telling us much, eh, Captain?"

"No, my lord. However," Guyime inclined his head at the village, "this man's grave is back there. Yet he, as you see, is here."

"Someone dug him up," Galvin said, heavy features drawn in grim puzzlement. "Why?"

"Valuables?" Anselm suggested. "Grave robbing is a common pastime for my own peasants. Can't imagine why the locals would be any different."

Galvin shook his head. "I'd wager a good amount this man died poor, my lord."

"Rich or poor, he's still silent." Anselm grimaced and took a firmer grip on his reins. "Father Lothare will take a dim view of just leaving him to rot in the open. Get him back in the ground so the rites can be said and let's be off. By my reckoning the keep is only two more days march distant."

Before riding away, the knight paused to glance at Guyime, as if in expectation of criticism or protest. Upon receiving only a stare of bland acceptance, he nodded and spurred his destrier to a gallop.

"It might be best to spend a while scouting the country," Galvin said, eyes tracking his lord's horse then turning back to Guyime. "There's something ill about this."

"Surely," Guyime agreed. The squire's instincts were sound, but would also entail a delay in reaching the keep. Since beginning this march, the Cartographer's map had remained stubbornly unchanged except for the ugly blot beside the lake. Lately it had taken on an incremental, pulsing expansion. Guyime concluded that whatever awaited them at the end of this march was growing in power with each passing day. Nor did he doubt it connected with this old man and his empty grave.

"Yet," he added to Galvin, "it would be best to get solid walls betwixt us and the wilds before investigating further. It's always best to look to your own defence before sending forth scouts."

Galvin's brow remained furrowed, but he nodded in acquiescence before turning to the village, hands cupped around his mouth as he bellowed for soldiers to come and get this poor old bastard back in his grave.

They found more bodies the next day. As they drew nearer to Blackfyre Keep, the mostly flat landscape gave way to undulating hills which obstructed much of the ground ahead. Also, by noon the steady drizzle of previous days had become a hard pelting deluge, so Sir Anselm failed to spot the line of corpses until his horse's hoof crushed the skull of one laying directly in his path. His strident shout of alarm caused Galvin to order the company into a defensive circle, carts clustered together whilst the men-at-arms formed a tight perimeter, weapons pointed into the rain.

Guyime found Anselm dismounted and peering at the body of a girl no more than fifteen summers in age. Nearby, his destrier huffed steam from his nostrils and scraped his gore-covered hoof across the ground.

"She was just…lying there," Anselm said, suddenly appearing a good deal younger, face wan and eyes wide as they blinked away the rain. "I couldn't see…"

"She's been dead for days," Seeker said, nodding to the mottled flesh of the girl's arms. She was clad in the plain, hardy clothes typically worn by peasant women when working the fields. However, the violence that had claimed her life

was evident in the ripped fabric of her sleeves and bodice, the revealed flesh blackened with corrupted wounds.

"Are those bite marks?" Guyime asked Seeker.

"Teeth and claws," she said after a brief perusal of the body. "This one wasn't taken by an aged heart."

"What manner of beast does that?" Anselm wondered. Guyime saw how his hands clenched his reins with a fierce, white-knuckled grip. For a man who had often ridden to war, he appeared strangely disconcerted by the sight of violent death.

Seeker's face showed an uncharacteristic pitch of bafflement as she rose from the body. "The marks are unfamiliar. I've seen people clawed by rabid apes in similar fashion, but this is not that."

"Another one over here!" Lorweth called from a dozen yards to their right, his form rendered vague by the rain. Moving to him, they found his grisly discovery to consist of a youth of boyish features, also clad in a peasant's working garb. His face had suffered no injury but his torso was even more savaged than the girl's, fabric and flesh torn away with such ferocity that much of his ribcage lay exposed.

"Your worship," Lorweth said quietly, nodding to a third slumped, unmoving shape a few paces on.

Guyime reached over his shoulder to draw the sword. "Go right," he told the druid. "Lexius, Seeker, go with him. No more than a hundred paces then return here. Ultria, your lordship." He inclined his head at Anselm and gestured to the hazy slope left of the road. "If you would care to join me?"

A trek of a hundred pace revealed a total of sixteen bodies, all apparently fallen in a broad arcing line. Each corpse was similarly mauled and the bodies at the same stage of decomposition.

Squinting through the deluge, Guyime saw yet more curving away in a grim procession that appeared to have no end.

"It's as if they all collapsed at once," Orsena said. "But how could they, being so badly injured?"

"Dragged here and arranged, my lady," Anselm sniffed. "See the way they're set out? I'd guess they form a great circle, a grim border around the keep. It appears some unknown malevolence does not wish us to reach our destination."

Guyime saw a fair deal of fear in the knight's bearing, albeit well controlled. Also, his reasoning appeared sound enough. Perhaps he was no stranger to battle after all.

"So many," Orsena said, scanning the arcing procession of corpses.

"The Ravager's Black Ledger marks the Vale of Stillwater Lake as both prosperous and populous," Anselm replied. "A prize worth claiming."

"Ravager's Black Ledger?" Orsena enquired, casting a cautious glance at Guyime.

"After seizing the throne, the tyrant king ordered his chamberlain to compile a grand ordinance of his kingdom," Anselm explained. "A count of every subject, great or small, and their possessions, down to every last bean and blade of grass, so the story goes."

"A strangely astute act for so renowned a madman," Orsena observed, Guyime feeling the weight of her eyes upon him.

"Mad to be sure, my lady," Anselm agreed. "But also peerlessly greedy by all accounts. To tax a people, you must first learn what they own."

Guyime averted his gaze from Orsena's discomfiting scrutiny, quelling the urge to impart a history lesson. In truth, the object of the Black Ledger hadn't been efficient taxation but conscription. King Guyime had harboured ambitions of taking his crusade against the Risen Church beyond the borders of his newly acquired realm; the Ravager had intended to become the Conquerer.

"It was a vast project," Anselm went on, "continuing long after the Ravager had disappeared off to whatever well-deserved eternal torment awaited him. The name stuck, however, and, despite the passage of years, the Black Ledger remains the most accurate account of the Northern Kingdom."

Anselm fell silent, his face betraying both anger and disgust as he viewed the peasant bodies. "Prosperous land yields a grim harvest in troubled times," he sighed.

"Laying out so many is a lot of trouble to go to," Guyime pointed out, keeping any inflection from his voice. Mention of the Black Ledger raised a flood of distracting memories, for not all had welcomed the intrusion of the king's agents and the Ravager hadn't stinted in suppressing such resistance. "And labour for many hands. An enemy who commands such strength could simply have attacked us on the road."

"I did not come here unprepared, Captain," Anselm replied. "I've accrued many a tale of these eastern rebels. Their wiles are devious and legendarily vicious. I wouldn't put it past them to slaughter their own folk in such manner. Also, in doing so they deny me my rents and the crops to sustain us."

Anselm stiffened, a hard resolution showing in his gaze as it tracked along the line of bodies. "Yet, I will not be diverted," he said. "I swore on bended knee before the king and the Altar of the First Risen that I would hold Blackfyre Keep for one year, and that is what I will do."

Orsena raised an eyebrow at Guyime, her expression as pitying as it was scornful.

"We should return to the company, my lord," he said. "To reach the keep before nightfall will require some hard marching, and I've no desire to make camp in this downpour."

"No doubts, Captain?" Anselm asked. Although clearly a man made foolish by love, he was not completely shorn of insight. "No cautionary words for your employer?"

Guyime slid the sword into its sheath and shrugged before turning away. "You pay me for neither doubt nor caution."

Chapter Five

The Blackfyre Crypt

Mercifully, the rain thinned and faded by the time they crested the line of hills that brought them within sight of the Vale of Stillwater Lake. On the far shore, Blackfyre Keep rose like a dark stump from the centre of a teardrop-shaped isthmus extending into the mirror-like surface of the lake. The land beyond the isthmus was a gently sloping expanse of enclosed pasture and densely wooded slopes dotted here and there with houses and barns. Guyime saw no smoke rising from the buildings and the fields were bare of livestock. Also, in accordance with Lakorath's observation, the air was absent any bird calls.

"Even the Execration was not so void of life," Seeker murmured, concern showing in the cast of her eyes as they tracked over the silent view. "Did Ekiri find it this way or make it so?"

"Questions still unanswered," Guyime reminded her. "Perhaps she waits for us in the keep."

"She doesn't. Nothing living resides here." Seeker lowered her head in momentary sorrow before straightening and starting down the slope. "Once again, Pilgrim, we're too late."

"Too late for what?"

Turning, Guyime found Galvin standing nearby. The squire had dismounted and the rain-softened earth concealed the sound of his approach. Yet Lakorath, Guyime assumed due to demonic mischief, had failed to warn him of the man's presence.

"The Rite of the Hunter's Moon," Guyime replied in bland dishonesty. "A sacred ritual amongst her people, one that can only be observed at a journey's end."

"Who's Ekiri?" a plainly unconvinced Galvin persisted. He came closer, hand tightening on the hilt of his sword, face darkening with burgeoning suspicion.

"One of the Beast Charmer gods." An outrageous lie, since Seeker's people tended to take violent exception to the notion of worshipping any god. "She hopes to placate them with a successful hunt."

"You've a skilled tongue when it comes to untruth, Captain." Galvin's temper showed in the clipped rasp of his voice and unwavering stare. "But don't mistake me for a low-born dolt. What is your true purpose here? I've seen the purses your band carries. You've no need of riches, and I'd wager the scholar and that high-born woman have never soldiered in their lives. You're no more a mercenary band than I'm a jackanapes."

Guyime gestured to the soundless landscape. "But your lord, to whom you are so very devoted, remains in dire need of swords. Now more than ever. And if you can't see that, then you are a dolt."

Galvin's lips twitched as he contained a snarl, eyes flicking to Anselm. The knight was engaged in affording his soldiers some good-humoured encouragement, waving them towards the keep with a hearty call: "Just another mile or two then we'll have a feast, eh, lads?"

"I'll tolerate no threat to him," Galvin grated. "Whatever your true reason for coming here, if it endangers him in any way, know that I will kill you, Captain."

Lakorath would normally have piped up with a cheerful suggestion of bloody murder at this point, but he either sensed no threat in the squire or found the confrontation beneath his notice. It happened sometimes. When the demon grew bored or distracted by his vast well of memories, the concerns of mortal kind became tiresome and unworthy of comment.

Guyime was similarly unperturbed by Galvin's promise. It had been more years than he could easily count since he had feared human violence. "What is it between you?" he asked, eyes shifting between the knight and the squire's flushed features. "Were you boyhood friends? The son of a castle scullion who became playmate to the lord's heir, perhaps? Is that what bound you together?"

"Battle bound us, hireling." Galvin abandoned his attempt to keep the snarl from his lips, taking a half-step towards Guyime, ugly promise writ large in his glower. "A knight who risks his life to save a lowborn youth pressed into line with scant knowledge of how to even hold a halberd, that knight is worthy of my service."

"Even when his hopeless devotion to a cruelly indifferent woman leads you here?"

Something changed in Galvin's bearing then, a shift behind his eyes that told of a barb finding its mark. "Lady Elsinora is not cruel," he rasped. "Do not speak of her again." The squire took another step closer. "And as for Sir Anselm, if he led me into the Infernus itself I'd follow..."

"Galvin!" Sir Anselm's call cut through the squire's threat. He plodded his destrier towards them, gesturing at the hill behind with weary impatience. "One of the carts has stuck in the mud on the far slope. See to it, would you?"

Galvin, his face now rigidly bare of emotion, spared Guyime a carefully blank stare before affording Anselm a short bow. "At once, my lord," he said, striding away.

Blackfyre Keep had been constructed along ambitious lines, its walls far taller than many a castle raised even by the richest lords. Guyime, no stranger to castles, reckoned its height arose from the confines of the isthmus upon which it sat. The long-vanished Baron Blackfyre, or more likely, his hired architect, had evidently seen the wisdom of building up where they couldn't build out. Consequently, the castle retained a good deal of its majesty despite the depredations of many years neglect. Yet, as they traversed the narrow spit of land separating keep from shore, Guyime saw clearly that its imposing walls were merely a facade for what was, undeniably, a ruin.

The baron's builders had rightly seen little utility in digging a ditch to the front of the main gate, since the constricted nature of the approach would spell doom for any attacking force. However, the gate itself was gone, great rusted iron hinges in the brickwork the only evidence of its prior existence. Beyond lay a lower courtyard rich in moss-covered stone and sprouting weeds. It surrounded a bailey consisting of a narrow, rectangular tower. The outer walls were tumbled in many places, creating deep, jagged ravines in the battlements. However, the inner tower appeared to retain its original height. Guyime concluded the outer walls had served to deflect the worst of the elements, protecting the tower's foundations and saving it from a shattering fall.

Despite this, a brief glance was enough to convince him that Blackfyre Keep was an indefensible relic requiring a year or more of repairs before it could hope to repel even a minor assault.

"Magnificent!" Sir Anselm enthused upon guiding his mount through the vacant arch of the gate. Once again his youth became apparent as he gazed around at his new holdfast, eyes bright. "Stands taller than any castle in the west, wouldn't you say, Galvin?"

"That I would, my lord."

"Some careful labour," Anselm went on, dismounting and tugging his leather gloves from his hands, "and I fancy this will do very well indeed." He turned to Guyime with a raised eyebrow. "Eh, Captain?"

Had honest counsel been his object, Guyime would have told this earnest knight errant to abandon this place and go home. If he was intent on staying, then felling trees and raising a wooden stockade atop the tallest nearby hill would have served him better than cloistering his force in this tumbledown trap. However, since honesty was not required here, Guyime's reply was anything but.

"Careful labour indeed, my lord," he agreed with a sage nod. "With your permission, my band will make a close inspection of the castle. Lexius has a peerless eye for architecture and will furnish a list of the most urgently needed works by morning."

"Excellent." Anselm slapped his gloves to his palm. "Whilst I shall tour the battlements for a time. Get a lay of the land, eh? Galvin, see to the disposition of the men and make sure you put a stop to any more fearful grumbling. I've been hearing too much of that lately."

"I'll see to it, my lord." The squire's response was prompt and brisk, although his narrowed gaze lingered on Guyime as he spoke. "Close inspection, is it?" he enquired when Anselm strode off to mount the steps to the broken battlement. "Looking for something?"

"Merely to do my paymaster's bidding." Guyime returned Galvin's stare with one of his own. This man's clever insights were becoming intrusively tiresome. "You have your orders, squire."

Galvin spared him a glower of understated rage before turning to assail a cluster of men-at-arms with a flurry of commands. Guyime ensured he was out of earshot before beckoning to Lexius and the others.

"Whatever the map led us to is likely to be in there," Guyime said, nodding to the tower. "It would be best if none of our comrades witnessed the finding. Master Druid, be so good as to loiter here, and conjure a distracting gale or two if any stray too close before we return."

"And once we've found it?" Orsena asked. "Whatever it might be."

"It's a sword," Seeker stated, features hard and voice flat with disappointment. "If Ekiri came here, she didn't stay. I'd know if she had. He expects to find another sword."

"Even so," Orsena said. "My question stands."

"Once we claim the sword," Guyime said, "we will have what we came for and the map will reveal our next steps which,

I'm sure," he paused to offer Seeker an encouraging grimace, "will lead us to Ekiri."

"Meaning we just take it and leave these men to their fate." Orsena's smooth brow took on a judgemental crease. "Having accepted coin to ensure their protection. It requires no magical insight to see that there's an ill-omen to this place. The very air stinks of doom. I may not be a natural-born child of Atheria, your highness, but I am still Atherian. In my city, a contract means something."

"Yes," Guyime returned. "Usually it means servitude and exploitation by a caste above all laws. We are not in your city now, Ultria, and these men would have met their fate without any assistance from us. Our shared mission is above one knight's lovelorn delusions."

He turned to Lorweth, not allowing her the interval to reply. "Master Druid, keep watch."

The tower's interior was predictably gloomy and required the lighting of torches to find their way.

"Stairwells and upper floors appear to be intact, at least," Lexius observed. The torchlight gleaming on his lenses gave him an owlish appearance as he made a tour of the hall that occupied the building's lowermost tier. "Sturdier construction than anything in Carthula," he added, running a hand over walls crafted from boulder-sized slabs of dark granite. "This could stand forever."

"Nothing stands forever," Guyime told him. "Live long enough and you get to witness once-great statues and temples fall to dust."

"Or once-unified kingdoms subside into war and lawlessness," Orsena commented in pointed annoyance. He couldn't tell if her pique arose from her ethical quandary or finding herself no longer occupying a position of unquestioned authority.

"Quite," Guyime said, deciding there was little need to antagonise her further. He raised his torch higher, revealing more of their surroundings. He recognised it as the main chamber of this keep, the place where the long-extinct Barons of Blackfyre had once convened council or heard petitions from bondsmen and peasants. The fine tapestries that once adorned the walls were now surely just dust on the flagstones, along with the long tables and chairs where family retainers feasted. Guyime's own chamber had been of larger dimensions, for his family had not been lacking in wealth, yet the similarity stirred an unexpected pang of memory.

He recalled how Loise had delighted in preparing the feasts, a task he was happy to leave in her hands since he found it so tedious. She would pay special attention to the seating arrangements, placing longtime friends in careful proximity to sometime enemies. In other castles this might have resulted in conflict, but few were roused to anger in Loise's company for she possessed a gift for resolving even bitter disputes with just a few words. Castle Matthile had been his to rule, but anything of worth that ever happened within its walls was the fruit of his wife's labour. Not that it saved her from the stake and the flames.

"There's another stairwell here," Lexius said, torch revealing a narrow doorway and a descending set of stone steps. Guyime found himself grateful for the scholar's echoing voice for it staunched the impending flood of memories.

"So," Orsena said, pursing her lips as she contemplated the stairwell before glancing at the ceiling. "Down or up?"

"Down," Guyime said, stepping through the doorway. "It's always down."

The stairwell described a gradual curve as it descended into the bowels of the keep. Long experience of underground places stirred expectations of thick cobwebs and scurrying rats, but, when the stairs ended and opened out into a low-ceilinged chamber, it transpired that the vaults of this place were as lifeless as the rest of it.

"The crypt of the Blackfyre family, I assume," Lexius said as the combined light of their torches revealed a row of sarcophagi. The lid of each bulky stone box was adorned with a carved relief of a knight clutching a sword, the nearest being the most accomplished in its craftsmanship.

"The ghostly Lord Orwin's father," Lexius mused, eyes tracking over the crest above the bearded stone features.

Guyime felt a small flare of disappointment at this. Since beginning this journey he had entertained the notion that Sir Lorent Athil might have fulfilled his long-cherished dream of coming here to claim the cursed keep. Perhaps that most noble soul had made himself lord of this land and found the peace that eluded him in life. Now it was clear that, if Lorent had ever come here, he hadn't felt minded to stay, not that Guyime found it surprising. Bereft of the beautiful and fierce Lady Ihlene, Lorent would ever be a lost and unsettled soul.

"If this place is home to ghosts and spectres," Orsena said, casting a glance at their shadowed surroundings, "this would seem the mostly likely spot for them to linger."

Guyime moved further into the crypt, eyes slipping from one abstract confluence of light and gloom to another. He had felt the touch of phantoms before yet sensed no such chill here. Even so, there was an undeniable weight to the air, a discomfiting itch that told of proximity to unseen, perhaps unknowable threats.

"It could be no more than a weaving of age-old fable, my lord," Lexius suggested, crouching to inspect the words etched into the side of the sarcophagus. "And we find ourselves in just an empty ruin."

"It's not empty," Guyime insisted. "The map wouldn't have brought us here for nothing." He watched Lexius move from one stone tomb to another, magnified eyes busily drinking in every inscription. "Anything of note?"

"Lists of battles," the scholar replied in a distracted murmur. "Lists of wives and children. No mention of fabled swords or demons."

"Of course not." Orsena gave a wry laugh. "That would be far too easy."

"If I were to hide a sword," Guyime said, resting a hand on the tomb of the most recently deceased Baron Blackfyre, "here seems a likely place, especially in the crypt of a famously haunted keep."

Orsena exchanged a wordless glance with him before moving to the opposite end of the sarcophagus. "It would seem wise," she said, grasping the edge of the stone lid, "to discuss what will be done with a demon-cursed blade should we actually find it."

"We shall claim it," Guyime replied simply.

"In order to claim it, you need to wield it," she pointed out. "And we are both intimately acquainted with the consequences of doing that."

"This mission is my burden most of all. If another hand is required to wield the next sword, it will be mine."

"Do you really think you will be able to abide having the voices of two demons in your head?"

"If I can abide this one, I can abide anything."

Guyime paused in expectation of Lakorath's caustic rejoinder. The demon, however, said nothing. Whilst Lakorath could be prone to prolonged silence, it occurred to Guyime that this particular sulk was considerably longer than usual. If anything was to stir him to comment it was the prospect of sharing occupancy of a mortal mind with another demon.

"Wait," he said as Orsena braced herself to shift the lift. Reaching over his shoulder, Guyime drew the Nameless Blade from its sheath. The revealed steel gleamed in the torchlight, yet possessed none of the faint but persistent thrum of power nor any vestige of a glow.

"Has she spoken to you recently?" he asked Orsena, nodding to the Conjurer's blade at her hip.

"Not for a time," she said. "I found it something of a blessed relief..." She trailed off as realisation began to dawn, drawing the curved short sword and running a tentative hand along the blade. "Nothing," she murmured. "I sense nothing."

"Lexius?" Guyime turned to the scholar, finding him standing nearby, small form rigid and hand shaking as it rested on the hilt of the Kraken's Tooth.

"I thought," he said, throat working to push the words out despite his obvious distress. "I thought she might be...resting."

Guyime's gaze snapped back to the Nameless Blade. It was a fine and ancient thing to look upon, edge keener than any razor and perfectly balanced, but now amounted to no more than a length of sharpened steel. A laugh rose to his lips but, for reasons he couldn't divine, failed to blossom into sound. For so long he had wished to be free of the voice contained in this thing, yet now he found the sensation unnerving. He had always expected this moment to feel like liberation; instead he was beset by the uncomfortable sense of being cast adrift.

"What is it?" Seeker asked, frowning in bafflement at her three companions.

"It appears," Orsena replied, "that our swords are now just…swords."

"An artefact of the curse upon this place," Guyime said. "Or some form of incantation. It has to be. A ward against demon magic, perhaps."

"Calandra is not a demon," Lexius pointed out. He had drawn the Kraken's Tooth now, the sword resting on his upturned hands as he regarded the inert metal.

"Some vestige of the demon she displaced must linger in the sword," Guyime said. "That's what enables her to bind her own soul to it. It's my guess that whilst we remain here the power contained in our swords is quelled." Another thought occurred as he continued to contemplate the sword in his hand, the sword he couldn't drop, nor cast away, no matter how hard he tried, not for decade upon decade.

Closing his eyes, he drew a breath then opened his hand.

Nothing. No clang of metal upon stone, no rush of exhilaration. Re-opening his eyes, he saw his hand still clutching the sword's handle. Gritting his teeth, he tried again, arm quivering with the effort of attempting to force his fingers open, to no avail.

"The demons and their magic may be silenced," he sighed in bitter realisation. "But the curse that binds them to us is not."

"How can that be?" Orsena wondered, her own sword still sitting firmly in her grasp despite a frantic effort to shake it loose.

"The demons didn't curse themselves," Lexius said. "Nor did Calandra. What holds their essence in these blades was crafted by a different hand. That magic is not affected by whatever spell reigns here."

The scholar's magnified eyes glowed with worry as he met Guyime's gaze, tears welling behind the curved glass of his lenses. "We cannot linger in this keep, my lord. I cannot be shorn of my wife. Not a second time."

"You won't be," Guyime promised him, sheathing the Nameless Blade and returning his attention to the sarcophagus. "We claim what we came for then we depart this place with all despatch. Ultria," he gestured to Orsena, "if you wouldn't mind?"

Thanks mostly to Orsena's inhuman strength, assisted marginally by Guyime, the lid was swiftly scraped aside to reveal the armour-clad bones within. The skull of Baron Blackfyre grinned up at them with yellowed teeth and vacant eyes beneath a helm of archaic design and, clutched in the overlapping, rusted gauntlets resting on his chest, there lay a sword.

Old bones and ancient plate scattered as Guyime reached into the tomb to draw the sword free of its master's grip. "Just a plain knightly longsword," he muttered in disappointment, drawing the weapon from its cracked leather sheath.

"If demon magic is quelled here," Lexius said, "how could we tell if this sword is cursed or not?"

"We can't," Guyime conceded. "But this pattern is too recent. Every one of the Seven Swords so far discovered has been of clearly ancient origin. Also," he turned the blade, allowing the light of Lexius's torch to reveal the rust spotting the metal, "they never age nor tarnish. This isn't it." He grunted in frustration, tossing the sword back onto the disordered bones of its former owner.

"There are other tombs," Orsena pointed out. "No doubt housing other swords."

A nagging intuition told Guyime that inspection of the remaining sarcophagi would yield much the same result. However, for want of another trail to follow, he nodded and started towards the next tomb, halting when a new voice filled the crypt with a roar of strident accusation.

"Have you come so far just to desecrate the dead?!"

Father Lothare's bearded visage was a picture of clerical anger as he strode into the light. Beyond him Guyime saw Lorweth descending the steps, hand held to his nose.

"Man's got a fast fist for a priest, your worship," the druid explained in nasal contrition. "Can't summon a gale when you're on your arse."

"This concerns you not, Father," Guyime said, jerking his head at Lothare in dismissal. "Get out of here."

"What vile mischief is this?" an undeterred Lothare demanded, looking into the opened tomb with both curiosity and righteous fury writ large on his features. "Hoped to steal yourselves some treasure, did you? How dare you abuse the remains of one buried in accordance with the church's rites?"

Had Lakorath still been able to offer advice, Guyime was sure it would have taken the form of a wincing admonition against immediate violence. The demon's silence, however, unshackled its host in more ways than one. This pestilent hypocrite's outrage was like a candle to the constantly smouldering tinder of Guyime's store of grievance, and now there was no chiding imp to stay his hand.

"I'll take no lessons on right or wrong from your kind," Guyime hissed in a low whisper. He started towards Lothare, the itch in his hands becoming a burn. For this one he would forsake the sword in favour of the dark satisfaction of an intimate strangling. When still a king, choking the life from captive priests had been a frequent amusement.

"Guyime!" Orsena's voice was sharp as she stepped into his path. "What is wrong with you?" She stared into his eyes with fearful inquisition, as if beholding a stranger.

His first impulse was to shove her aside, but one touch to her shoulder reminded him that she, although a foot or more shorter than he, was no more moveable than a granite wall. "I'll not suffer judgement," he told her, the ancient rage boiling now, like a sickness in the way it churned his guts and put a tremble in his limbs. "Not from a priest…"

Further discord would surely have ensued if not for the sudden if muted clamour of raised voices from above. Louder still was the pealing of a horn followed shortly by the call of Galvin's voice echoing down the stairwell. "Captain! Get your dogs up here! You're needed!"

Chapter Six

Eyes of Green Fire

The soldier's face was frozen, almost corpse-like in its paleness and immobility save for the blinking of wide, terrorised eyes. He sat on a barrel in the courtyard, heedless of the brandy flask Father Lothare held to his lips and also deaf to all questions.

"It's all fine, Iervo," the priest prompted with soft reassurance. "You're safe now, lad. Have a drink. Take your time in telling the tale."

However, Iervo, a strapping man with the scars and well-worn brigandine of a veteran man-at-arms, seemed incapable of telling any tale. Nor did he appear to heed the sound of his own name. In any case, Guyime felt the man's story was rendered superfluous by the copious gore that covered him. From the chest down, his garb was dark with blood and spattered with both flesh and bone.

"How many men did you send with him?" Guyime asked Galvin.

"Just two," the squire said. "Aginor and Franick. A short walk to the woods on the lakeshore to gather firewood."

"Not short enough."

Guyime moved to the vacant arch of the gatehouse, staring at the sprawl of woodland fringing the shore beyond the isthmus. Night was fast approaching now, the trees a blank wall of anonymous shadow, just as silent as before. The lake was well named, for the surface betrayed barely a ripple to disturb the reflection of forest and sky.

"Any scent?" he asked as Seeker came to his side.

"She tastes fresh blood on the wind," the beast charmer said as Lissah's lithe form coiled about her legs, lips repeatedly drawing back to reveal her fangs. "And something else." Seeker's expression became guarded when Galvin and Anselm moved to join their survey of the ground beyond the keep.

"Corruption," Seeker said after Guyime gave her a nod of assent. "She senses dead things, like the old man pulled from his grave but worse, more rotted."

"I'd wager there's not a soul within ten miles by now," Galvin said, peering at the gloom-covered landscape. "Ambush then retreat. It's the way with rebels."

"No souls," Seeker agreed. "But something is out there, waiting, watching."

Guyime was unused to perceiving fear in this woman, but he saw it now in the shudder she failed to contain. "This is a trap, Pilgrim," she told him quietly. "A snare we have willingly walked into."

"Snares is it?" Anselm said. His face was dark with anger and he glared at the far shore with naked impatience. "No rebel will imprison me in my own keep. I'll have blood for my men, honest soldiers murdered by traitorous filth."

"Eaten, my lord." Iervo spoke in a toneless mutter, his expression unchanged. "They were eaten," he added, a faintly curious expression passing over his brow, as if he were recalling a joke with an unfunny conclusion.

"Eaten by what, lad?" the priest asked, but it appeared Iervo had exhausted any knowledge he was willing to share. Guyime had seen the faces of enough maddened men to know that no amount of patient coaxing would return this one to sanity.

"Best put a close watch on him," he advised Galvin before turning to Anselm. "My lord, any foray will have to await morning. Venturing forth at night into country we don't know only invites ambush. Come the dawn, with Seeker's help, we'll track the steps of whoever slew your men and visit necessary justice. In the meantime, I suggest we set watches to cover the gaps in these walls. Tomorrow, trees must be felled to create barricades and doors for this gate."

Anselm, for all his evident desire for retribution, was at least amenable to common sense. Watches of ten soldiers each were placed on the gaps in the walls, changed every three hours to allow a modicum of rest before sunrise. The company bedded down in the main chamber of the tower, with Anselm and the Stone Dogs occupying the upper floors. An inspection of the stairwells revealed a good deal of cracked masonry but the steps remained intact all the way to the top.

Climbing onto the tower's summit, Guyime found Lorweth sitting between two crenellations. He had an arm raised to the sky where a small cloud, lit by the crescent moon, formed a gently revolving spiral.

"Seems I remain immune to whatever malaise infects this place, your worship," he said brightly as Guyime moved to his side. "That's something, eh?"

Guyime rested his forearms on the stonework to gaze out at the placid lake water. "Druidic magic is highly distinct from the demonic, as I recall."

"Wouldn't know about that." Lorweth shrugged and let his arm fall to his lap, the small cloud above slipping into vapour. "Never had much've an education in the arcane arts, truth be told. The urge to wander claimed me at an early age, y'see? So off I went, without benefit of an elder's wisdom."

He spoke with typical off-hand humour, but Guyime had many years experience of perceiving mummery. "You're lying," he said. "I suspect your education was fairly comprehensive, but also harsh in nature. I've found that's often the way when it comes to learning anything of value."

He saw a small flush of resentful concern on the druid's face before he turned away. Habitual liars rarely appreciated the unravelling of their tales.

"I don't care, Master Druid," Guyime told him. "I don't harbour the slightest regard for your past or your assuredly long litany of misdeeds. I do care about the as yet unanswered question of why you continue to attach yourself to us. You bear no cursed sword, receive no pay, yet you are with us for every mile of the journey."

"I told you in Atheria, your worship." Lorweth shot him a wide smile notable for its patent insincerity. "There's a considerable debt betwixt us, and I aim to see it settled."

"No, that's not it. As I've told you several times, I consider your debt paid. What is it that draws you to this hunt, I wonder? It can't be a desire to claim one of the swords. You are not so foolish as to think possessing such a thing is anything but a curse. So why?" He leaned closer when Lorweth didn't answer, voice hardening in insistence. "Why?"

"Does it matter?" A rare blossoming of anger shone in Lorweth's eye as he turned to Guyime, one that reminded both that the balance of magic in their band had abruptly shifted. The druid was now the most powerful soul amongst them.

"It matters," Guyime said, refusing to be cowed, "because I suspect our survival here will depend a great deal on you. I have skills and battle-ken. Seeker is perhaps the finest archer I've ever seen. Lexius is wise beyond all others. Orsena is stronger than ten men. Yet without the power of our swords we sit as bait in this trap awaiting those set to feed upon us, and I've no doubt they're coming. What I wish to know from you, Master Druid, is will you stand when they do?"

The anger lingered in Lorweth's glare for a moment longer, fading as he blinked and shifted his gaze to the sky once more. "Threads," he said in a soft sigh. "That, your worship, is why I stay."

Guyime frowned in irritated bafflement. "Threads?"

"The term loses a good deal in translation from Mareth," Lorweth explained. "But that's the closest word in northtongue. The notion that there's a great web of unseen threads running through the stuff of the world lies at the heart of druidic lore. Mundane souls can never see nor sense it, but a druid can. We're only afforded glimpses, perhaps one or twice in a lifetime, just brief visions of one small part of something vast painted in all the colours of the rainbow, and more besides. Some threads are dark, others glow brighter than the sun. Each one leads somewhere and means something; a destiny, a danger, a blessing. My vision came that day on the sea, when you snatched me from the jaws of a shark. Just for an instant I saw the web, so many threads, entwined in endless complexity, but one in particular shining bright then dark, one that binds me to you. Why, I can't know. But I've a fancy I will, when the swords are found."

He closed his eyes and let out a long breath. "You ask why I stay with you." He paused to voice a mirthless chuckle. "That supposes I have any choice. When a druid catches hold of his thread, there's no letting go."

His story summoned the Cartographer's words when she gave Guyime the map, her allusions to the fate of the Seven Swords being etched into the fabric of the world. Lately, in the quieter hours of the night, he had begun to wonder if this search was destined to become as much a curse as the one it was intended to banish. *Is that what you're doing? Banishing a curse?* Had Lakorath's voice still been present he knew this would be the demon's archly phrased question. The truth was he had no true conviction that bringing the swords together would free him from the blade on his back. All he had were the words of the Mad God, a high-ranking demon certain to delight in lies. Yet, ever since the Cartographer unfurled her map he had known there was no turning from the path it revealed; he had his own thread.

"There'll be blood tomorrow," he told Lorweth, turning to descend the stairs. "Get some rest and be ready. We're not leaving without a sword."

Anselm insisted on setting forth astride his destrier, despite the fact that, as the only rider amongst their party, it clearly marked him as both leader and target.

"I fear no rebel arrow, Captain," he told Guyime, stiffening in offence before kicking his heels to send the warhorse trotting through the gate.

"Arrows don't recognise bravery," Guyime told Galvin who had charge of the dozen men-at-arms gathered for this foray. The remainder of the company were busily hammering felled timbers to fashion barricades and the makeshift doors that would seal the gate. Guyime entertained little optimism that they would complete either task by nightfall. "It would be best if you instilled some caution in our lord, squire," he added.

"Our lord is his own man," Galvin responded evenly before barking an order at the soldiers, setting them into motion at a fast march.

Guyime waited until Galvin was through the gate before turning to Orsena and Lexius. "Stay here and scour every inch of that crypt," he told them. "Open all the caskets and inspect every scrap of weaponry you find. If the priest voices any further objections, feel at liberty to break his neck and blame it on a fall down the stairs."

"I won't be doing that, your highness," Orsena assured him before giving a pointed glance at a second party formed around a canvas-wrapped bundle laying upon the courtyard flagstones. Father Lothare stood beside the bundle, head lowered as he recited the rites of the dead. "Besides, our clerical friend has another task to occupy him at present."

Guyime grunted in agreement. Galvin had followed his advice in placing the blank-faced Iervo under close watch. A few hours past midnight, however, the fellow had returned to some semblance of reason, speaking in sorrowful but calm tones of the comrades he had lost and their many battles together.

Feeling him to be mostly restored to his former self, the watchers had allowed him to visit the privy unescorted. Once behind the curtain, Iervo promptly took a hidden knife from his boot and slit his throat from ear to ear. Guyime harboured a growing certainty he would not be the last corpse to litter this keep, but he might well be the only one to die by his own hand.

"Stay atop the tower," he said, turning to Lorweth. "Keep a close watch."

The druid, unusually, had no words this morning and replied only with a terse nod. Guyime knew his reticence arose from their conversation the night before. Apparently, the mere act of speaking of his druidic insight was sufficient to sour his mood enough to still a busy tongue.

Guyime adjusted the sword belt slanting across his chest before nodding to Seeker. As the two of them followed in the wake of Galvin's party he reflected on the curious realisation that the sword felt heavier than ever.

"Soaked in blood, like the others," Seeker reported, pressing her fingers into the soil. "Older though."

They spent an entire day making a thorough inspection of the woods where Galvin had dispatched the unfortunate Iervo and his friends, finding no bodies but ample evidence of violent death. This forest was thick but also dotted with clearings and broken by inlets as it traced along the lakeshore. The clearings were home to numerous cottages and, in the inlets, small jetties and fishing boats bobbing in the gentle swell. Of their owners, however, there was no sign whilst the cottages were rich in shattered crockery and furniture, floors, walls and ceilings all besmirched by the signature dark brown of dried gore. This patch of bloodied ground was but one of several Seeker had discovered. Like the others it lay close to the shore, and save for a few fragments of bone or torn flesh, they could find no corpse.

"How much older?" Guyime asked her, eyes busy scanning the surrounding trees. He was only just realising how accustomed he was to Lakorath warning him of hidden dangers. Lord Anselm had seen fit to divide their party so as to more efficiently scour the shore. It was a foolhardy choice but Guyime hadn't objected, keen to hear Seeker's verdict clear of Galvin's inquisitive ears.

"Days." Seeker rose, surveying the ground with the particular focus that possessed her on the hunt. He assumed the unfound bleeder had come from the fishing settlement clustered around a narrow inlet a hundred paces away. Guyime could see Anselm guiding his destrier through the silent cottages with his half-dozen men.

"This one is the furthest from the lake so far," Seeker went on. "But not by much. And the blood." She swept a hand over the ground towards the placid waters visible through the matrix of pine and ash. "It always forms a trail to the shore."

"Killed and then dragged away to be dumped in the lake?" Guyime suggested. "Why bother when evidence of the crime is so plentiful?"

"Not dragged," Seeker said, nodding to a scrape in the earth a few yards off. "A footprint, one of many near each scene of death, always walking away."

There was a knowledge in the gaze she turned on him, one born of shared experience they hadn't yet voiced. However, before she spoke the word he knew had risen to her lips, it was rendered moot by the shrill, agonised scream echoing from the direction of the fishing settlement.

Seeker instantly unslung her bow and set an arrow to the string, starting towards the settlement in a crouching run, then pausing to glance back at him, puzzled by his failure to follow. "Pilgrim?"

Leave them to whatever horror lurks here. With the lordling dead, Galvin will be too stricken by grief to trouble himself with our plans. Thoughts that would have fit well in Lakorath's mouth, and yet they were entirely Guyime's own. *No,* he corrected himself. The cadence of these new, ugly suggestions was different, shot through with a gravelly timbre he had last heard when confronted with the shade of his former self in Atheria. *These are the Ravager's thoughts.*

"Pilgrim!" Seeker said again, voice taking on a urgent note as another scream came from the settlement. This was easily identifiable in its volume and shrillness as the death throes of a horse, a sound Guyime had heard on many a battlefield. Ancient pangs of self-hatred put a dark glower on his brow as he reached to draw the Nameless Blade and started towards the inlet at a steady run.

They found the first body slumped against a gutting shed near the jetty, one of Anselm's men-at-arms, his neck and face flensed down to bare muscle and bone. A single intact eye stared sightlessly at them as they hurried past, drawn to the cottages ahead by the tumult of yells and clamour of weaponry.

Guyime made for the gap between two dwellings then came to a skidding halt as something leapt from the thatched roof above to land in his path. He caught only a glimpse of chattering teeth in a blackened face, two eyes gleaming green in the gathering dusk, before the thing sprang at him.

Had the sword possessed its full demonic power, the blow he delivered would have severed his assailant clean in two at the waist. Instead it hacked only halfway through the torso, cleaving through rotted rags and grey flesh to shatter the spine. Guyime kicked it away, gagging on the stench of sundered bowels as it came free of the blade. The creature landed on its back and immediately began to thrash, a sound that mingled a retch with a hiss emerging from its snapping maw. However, its eyes were what captured Guyime's attention, their emerald glow bright but still somehow ugly, hateful.

"Dritch wight!" Seeker grunted, stepping forward to slash through the thing's neck with her long-bladed knife. As the blade parted the head from the body, the light in its eyes flickered and died. Shorn of animation, the thing became just a corpse, revealed as that of a girl perhaps thirteen years old.

"No," Guyime said. "Their eyes don't glow like that. And you saw how it moved. Wights shamble, they don't leap. This is something else."

The despairing, dwindling yell of a human death cry drew them on. Guyime turned a corner to find Anselm alone beside the body of his half-eaten destrier. The bodies of his men-at-arms lay around him, suffering the attentions of several more green-eyed figures. Anselm's sword swung to and fro as he fended off a group of five in varying states of decay, all clad in the damp, wasted remnants of fisherfolk. As with the girl Guyime had cut down, their eyes all shone with a burning green fire.

Charging forward, Guyime lopped the head from a wight busily gorging itself on the throat of a slain soldier before slicing the legs away from a stocky woman assailing Anselm. As she fell, he reversed the blade and stabbed the point through her brow, grunting in satisfaction at the sight of the green glow guttering then fading in her eyes.

"The head, my lord," he told Anselm as the knight thrust his sword through the chest of a large man with but one arm and a bundle of guts leaking from his belly like a nest of grey snakes. The one-armed man stiffened and fell when Seeker's arrow pierced him from nape to nose.

"You have to take the head," Guyime added by way of emphasis, hacking his way to Anselm's side. Even shorn of demon magic, the Nameless Blade remained keen as ever, although slicing through three skulls in quick succession required considerably more effort than usual. The remaining two creatures, seemingly enraged by this interruption, rose from their feasting to come at Guyime and Anselm in a ravening rush, the same guttural hiss emerging from their throats. Both fell to Seeker's arrows before they came within reach of their swords.

"They just…appeared," Anselm stammered, wiping a spattering of dark gore from his face. "Rose up from the grass. My men…" He gaped at the corpses littering the ground before turning to his destrier. "My horse."

Hearing a sibilant chorus from the direction of the nearby woods, Guyime saw a dozen more figures separate from the shadowy backdrop of the trees. They approached slowly at first, their sure-footed, part-hunched litheness a predatory contrast to the mass of wights Guyime and Seeker had battled in the Execration. All eyes glimmered with the same viridescent glow, which at least enabled Guyime to gauge the distance despite the gathering dusk. A flicker of green off to the right revealed yet more on the shore, forms glistening as they emerged from the water.

"You were right," Guyime muttered, turning to Seeker as she moved to his side, bow trained on the oncoming foe. "They wait in the lake during daylight, emerge at sunset to claim more victims."

"What are they?" Anselm breathed. Although plainly attempting to master the twinned ailments of terror and shock, the knight hadn't run. *No coward at least,* Guyime thought with grudging admiration.

"Something beyond my considerable experience," he told Anselm in gruff honesty. "Which we lack the numbers to fight at present. I suggest speedy withdrawal to the keep, my lord."

He saw a prideful reluctance bunch the knight's features before he grimaced and nodded. However, as he began to back away in concert with Guyime and Seeker, he paused, eyes widening as he made out one particular figure amongst the oncoming horde. It stood taller than the others and was clad in a soldier's brigantine, albeit torn and ripped from shoulder to hip.

"Aginor?" Anselm asked, taking an involuntary step forward.

"Hold!" Guyime snapped, latching a hand to the knight's arm.

"But, I know this man," Anselm said. "He marched under my father's banner as he marches under mine…"

Anselm's words faded when Aginor came to a halt twenty paces away. His features were a pallid half-mask. One side retained the grey, part-sagging flesh of a recently deceased man, the other a blackened, ruined mess around a socket that lacked an eye yet still emitted a green glow. The former man-at-arms raised his head a little, jaw widening to issue a sound that differed from the sickening hiss Guyime had heard from the others. This was more rhythmic, a steady, thick clacking he recognised as a parody of human laughter.

"Kill it!" Guyime instructed Seeker, but before she could raise her bow the thing that had been Aginor slipped onto all fours with unnatural swiftness. He became a shadow in the grass, moving too fast to track. Beyond him the rest of the creatures mimicked his example, crouching then loping forward in a charging mass. Seeker's bowstring thrummed and Guyime saw one tumble head over heels then lay still, but there were a good deal more.

"Back to back," Guyime told Anselm and Seeker, knowing there was no chance to run. These things moved too fast to allow an escape. "Remember, my lord..."

"The head," Anselm said, raising his sword as the three of them formed a tight cluster. "I know."

They cut down the first rush in a brief frenzy of slashing blades whilst Seeker's bow claimed another before she drew her long knife and stabbed it through the head of a portly man lacking a lower jaw. Guyime jerked the sword free of an old woman's skull and kicked her stick-like body away, levelling the blade in expectation of another charge. The green-eyed dead, however, appeared content to circle them for now. Emerald orbs blinked as they prowled through the grass whilst their collective hiss rose to an aggravating pitch.

"Not mindless," Guyime observed, something else that set these abominations apart from other wights.

"Like lions, or hyenas," Seeker agreed, her bow once again primed with an arrow, stave creaking as she tightened the string. "Circle the prey, wait for an opening."

"Rebel devilry has conjured this foulness," Anslem asserted. The strident resolve in the knight's voice was contrasted by the way he gagged as a gobbet of foul-smelling ordure dripped from his sword hilt to his hand. He flicked it away with a gasp of fearful disgust.

"Devilry to be sure," Guyime said. "But I'd wager you won't find a rebel within a hundred miles of this place."

The next attack came without warning. A spindly youth, naked save for the ragged shirt that partly covered his torso, sprang from the grass directly at Anselm. The boy's clacking jaws and lashing of clawed hands ended abruptly when Seeker's arrow skewered his head.

"Trying to panic the herd," she grunted, nocking another shaft to her bowstring, eyes scanning the undergrowth.

The failure of this assault appeared to stir the rest of the pack to anger, their accumulated hissing growing louder, the grass swaying with greater energy. Guyime needed no demonic insight to know whatever drove them, be it hunger or malice, was about to overtake their predatory caution.

"Keep together…" he began, drawing the sword back level with his head for a swift strike. His next words were swallowed by a chorus of yells from the direction of the fishing village. Raising his eyes from the grass he saw Galvin leading his men towards them in a charge. The squire moved with a swiftness the belied his size, both hands clutching an iron-studded mace that he promptly used to good effect, smashing the skull of the creature that rose to bar his path.

Seeing the creatures surrounding them break their circle and surge to meet the new threat, Guyime was quick to seize the advantage. He and Seeker had fought alongside one another with enough frequency for him to communicate his intention with a brief touch to her shoulder before starting forward, pace fast but measured.

"Follow, my lord!" he called to Anselm as he plunged into the grass, sword whirling to cut open the head of a brawny fisherman intent on charging Galvin. The creatures had swiftly fixed upon the squire as the most potent threat, a dozen or more closing upon him as he swung his mace with furious industry. Guyime saw him crack the skulls of three attackers before a fourth, a small child scrambling with monkey-like quickness, leapt onto the squire's back. Galvin roared in pain and rage as the infant clamped its small jaws on his neck, worrying like a terrier at a rat hole. With the squire distracted by the attack, the other creatures surged to finish him. Fortunately, Guyime had closed the distance by the time their hands clamped onto Galvin's studded jerkin, scratching and clawing. A few deft strokes of the Nameless Blade left a trio of twitching corpses on the ground, the green fire guttering from their eyes. Reaching over his shoulder, Galvin tore the still-biting child clear of his neck, casting it into the air to be spitted by Anselm's sword.

"Galvin!" The knight rushed to his squire's side, staring at his wound with distressed concern.

"Not…" Galvin grunted, staggering a little before straightening his back, one hand clamped to the bite marks. "Not so bad, my lord."

"Drawing back," Seeker observed, Guyime turning to see the creatures had retreated into the grass. The emerald glint of their eyes flicked into small specks that faded towards the treeline, where they lingered, watching. "Like lionesses when they lose some of their number to the buffalos' horns."

"Then let's not await the next hunt," Guyime said, looking to Anselm. "To the keep, my lord?"

The Anselm of yesterday might have argued. However, this youthful knight with his wide, moist eyes and patent fear for Galvin, voiced no protest as they gathered the five surviving men-at-arms and made haste to Blackfyre Keep with all the speed they could muster.

Chapter Seven

The Besieging Dead

The squire's steps began to falter when they neared the keep, his skin slicking with foul-smelling sweat and his breath taking on a ragged grate. Anselm and Guyime were obliged to drag him across the isthmus and by the time they bore him through the gate he was barely conscious.

"My lord..." he slurred as Anselm called loudly for Father Lothare. "The barricades...need seeing to..."

Lothare greeted them in the courtyard, working a red-stained rag over the gnarled head of his hefty walking stick. "Iervo was dead," he explained. "Then he wasn't. We burned the body."

He pressed a hand to the squire's damp brow, grunting, "Lay still, you mighty oaf." From the quickness with which he drew back his touch, Guyime divined the depth of Galvin's fever went far beyond the norm. "Get him inside," Lothare said, jerking his head at the nearby men-at-arms and gesturing to the tower.

"My lord," Guyime said as Anselm began to follow the priest. "You must look to your keep."

"What?" Anselm demanded, brow creased with a mingling of noble outrage and resented distraction.

"Your keep," Guyime repeated, softly but precisely, stepping closer to the knight. "Your men." He cast a pointed glance around the courtyard where soldiers stood watching in either abject fear or mystification. Iervo's rising and Galvin's wounding had wrought a dire effect on their courage. "They require leadership. These walls and this gate must be sealed."

"Galvin…" Anselm said, turning back to the tower.

"Your keep," Guyime cut in. "The one you swore to hold. If you don't lead these men, it falls tonight and they with it."

The anger lingered on Anselm's face as he returned Guyime's stare until a grudging shadow of understanding passed across his gaze. "Sergeant-at-arms Tuhmel!" he called out, breaking the contest with Guyime and moving away.

One of the onlooking soldiers straightened, a stocky, heavy-jawed man a few years older than his comrades. "My lord!"

"The state of our defences?" Anselm asked him, voice clipped with a new terseness.

"Timbers readied, my lord," Tuhmel said. "Reckon we've got enough to raise five-foot walls in the breaches. Only enough to half seal the gate, though. Was waiting for Squire Galvin's word on how to proceed."

"Wait no longer," Anselm told him. "I want all barricades raised by midnight. And get our archers on the battlements. They're to call out at the first sign of anything approaching this keep, no matter how strange it may appear. And tell them to watch the lake as well as the shore."

The sergeant's anvil-like jaw worked a little as the man considered his next words, exchanging glances with his men, all pale of face and uncertain of bearing. "If I may, my lord," he said. "What's out there? Is it the same as what befell Iervo?"

Seeing Anselm's brow furrow as he struggled to find a reply that wouldn't raise the fears of these soldiers to a yet higher pitch, Guyime said, "It's the same thing that sits outside the walls of any castle under siege." He moved to place a firm hand on the sergeant's shoulder, making sure the man saw the command in his eyes. "Something that wants to kill you. Now, if you're keen to see the dawn, save your questions and follow your liege lord's commands."

Father Lothare's face was grim as he pressed the poultice to Galvin's wound, the priest's gaze shadowed by something Guyime had seen on many a healer's face.

"It's a form of corruption I've never seen the like of before," Lothare said, rising from the stricken man's side. He moved to a cask of clean water, dipping a pus- and blood-stained cloth into it before wringing it out on the stone floor. He glanced over his shoulder at Galvin's bulky, inert form laid out on a bed of straw sacks in the tower's main chamber. "Turned the wound black in the space of an hour. Spreads too fast for gangrene. Smells a good deal fouler too."

"Medicines," Anselm said, his voice shot through with a hoarse, demanding note. "Balms..."

"There's no balm nor physick known to man that would cure this, my lord," Lothare told him. "The corruption is in his veins now, his bones too most likely. Truth be told, it's only thanks to the sheer brute strength of the man that he hasn't died already. I'm sorry. All we can do now is ease his pains and pray to the Risen for his soul."

Anselm's features took on the blankness Guyime knew signified a man confronting something both horrible and inescapable. The knight's lips twitched as yet more desperate pleas stirred his tongue only to fade in the face of Lothare's implacable visage.

"A tour of the keep is in order, my lord," Guyime said. "Gauge the progress of the defences, maintain the men's spirits. I'll take Seeker to the top of the tower. Her cat sees well in the dark."

Anselm hesitated, eyes lingering on the squire who had begun to stir in feeble distress. "Elsinora," the knight said, voice faint. "She always had such a care for him. Telling her of this..." His voice faltered and he let out a sigh, tearing his gaze from Galvin. "Tour of the keep, Captain," he said, moving to the door. "Quite right."

Guyime watched him exit the tower before turning an intent stare upon Lothare. "You killed Iervo," he said. "Or rather the thing that had been Iervo. As a widely travelled man, I assume you know what will happen when the squire dies."

Lothare consented to meet his eye for only a second before reaching for a clean cloth from the chest that held his curatives. "I do," he said, voice clipped with evident reluctance.

"He's too big and strong to allow to rise and wreak havoc..."

"I know!" Lothare rounded on him, beard parting to reveal his teeth in an angry snarl. "Damn you, I know." His ire calmed quickly and he moved back to Galvin's side, voicing a bitter reply, "I'll see to it. But not an instant before it's needed. Now, leave me to my work."

"I've seen the dead brought to a semblance of life before, but not like this."

Guyime rested his hands on the edges of the Baron Blackfyre's tomb, meeting the eyes of each of his companions in turn. He wanted to ascribe the strain in his arms as he gripped the stone to his imagination, but it was too acute to be denied. Muscles that hadn't expressed the slightest ache for decades of wandering and battle now felt stretched, as if the long years of his unnaturally prolonged existence had suddenly decided to make themselves known. Also, an unfamiliar tug of weariness had started to cloud his mind, something he found irked him more than his bodily aches.

Without the demon, he thought, quelling the impulse to run a tired hand over his drooping brow, *what am I but a very old man with a sharp sword?*

Gritting his teeth against the mounting fatigue, he settled a questioning look on Lexius. "Bodies that should be wasted by corruption move with all the quickness and ferocity of a wolf," Guyime said. "Possessing eyes that glow with a green fire."

Throughout their acquaintance, Guyime had noted how Lexius seemed to be incapable of forgetting even the smallest scrap of lore. Typically, he answered all questions without pause, effortlessly plucking the required facts from his mental archive of arcane and ancient knowledge. Now, however, he allowed a notable interval before replying, one Guyime doubted had anything to do with a dulled memory.

"It's a fragmentary tale," the scholar said. As ever, the lenses he wore made it hard to gauge his mood, but there was no mistaking the foreboding in his voice. "One that was old before even the rise of eternal Valkeris. But at least it provides us the name of our quarry, and our foe. For, I suspect they are the same thing."

"The sword we seek is doing this?" Orsena asked him.

"I believe so." Lexius cast a frustrated gaze around the gloomy recesses of the crypt. "Somewhere in this structure there lies a blade that has many names, but the oldest strikes me as the most apt: the Necromancer's Glaive. As you know, Calandra's father was obsessed with the Seven Swords and set me to researching any and all tales regarding supposedly enchanted swords or blades. The vast majority are patent nonsense or invention, but always it was the most ancient and rare that ring the truest. Some could even be corroborated by other sources. So it was with the Necromancer's Glaive.

"On the northern shore of the third sea there sits a ruin, so ancient and denuded by time that many will perceive it only as a jumble of old stones rather than the great city it once was. Its name is lost, as is the language of the people who live there. All we have are the tales of its fall. The more rational scholars ascribe it a terrible pestilence that swept the Five Seas in ancient times, a sickness with no cure that raged for a year and claimed two-thirds of the population before it faded.

"The city on the shore was no exception, much to the distress of its king, for he greatly loved his people and the trials of watching them die drove him beyond madness. The pestilence was particularly fierce in his domain, sparing only a handful of people, including their maddened king who now reigned all but alone in a city of corpses. Raging and weeping he wandered the silent streets, imploring the dead to return, whereupon he found himself confronted by a living man, a stranger from far across the sea. A stranger bearing a sword.

"'If thou takest this blade,' the stranger told the mad king, 'and bargain with the beast that lurks within, then thine subjects will be restored unto thee.' And so the mad king took the sword from the stranger who promptly vanished, never to be seen again. The beast within the blade whispered its vile enticements to the king, promised him that all he need do was unleash the power of the blade and once again his people would walk the streets of this majestic city. But, as is the way with demons, there was a lie in the promise. For, when the king held forth the blade and summoned its power, his people rose, but they rose as the corpses they had become. The sword's evil magic filled them, making their eyes glow with the colour of the sickness that had claimed them. Great was their hunger and their malice, for they were driven by a demon's lust. Great was the destruction they wrought upon their city and great the slaughter when they spread beyond its confines to assail those of other lands. The mad king's army of death grew with every massacre, for in killing they swelled their number. The bite of one of these creatures is invariably fatal and all the dead within reach of the glaive's malice were cursed to walk and feast on the living.

"What happened next is vague. The various legends contradict each other. Some say that armies of mortal men were gathered to oppose this host of dire wights, as they came to be called, and eventually prevailed, killing the mad king and casting his cursed sword into the sea, or sometimes a volcano. Others state that it was the mad king himself who brought an end to the onslaught. By sheer power of will he returned himself to sanity and contained the demon's influence in the sword before taking himself off to die a lonely death in far off lands, far away from the province of men. There are a few scattered stories dating from earlier times, fables of the dead summoned from the grave to wreak havoc, but they are sparse. It seems that, for most of its existence, the power of the Necromancer's Glaive has been contained, until now."

"Someone unleashed it," Guyime said. He kept his gaze from Seeker but she had evidently already formed her own conclusion.

"Ekiri," she said. "My daughter came here weeks ago, this we know." She closed her eyes, jaws bunching. "She unleashed it, somehow. The dagger she carries, the thing inside it has enslaved her, set her to craft this trap for us."

"Meaning," Lorweth mused, "it knows we're tracking it."

"It didn't guide her here to claim a sword," Guyime realised. "But to draw us here, so that its power would end us." He let out a small, bitter laugh, knowing Lakorath would have surely described this piece of deadly cunning as worthy of the Ravager himself. He sobered quickly, sensing the others' discomfort at hearing him voice any expression of humour.

"If the ancient tale is true," he said, "then we know the power of the Necromancer's Glaive can be contained. As long it remains undiscovered anyone who dies within reach of its influence will rise and feast on the living."

"The line of bodies we found must mark the limit of its power," Orsena said. "But the village where the old man clawed his way out of the grave lies beyond that line."

"Magic is like a flame, your ladyship," Lorweth said. "Burns bright when it's first lit, then recedes. I'd guess the old man was awoken when the sword was found in this keep." He grimaced. "Wherever it might be hiding itself."

Orsena shook her head. "The tombs hold only rusted swords. We opened each one and checked every corner of this crypt. It's not here."

"It must be..." Guyime insisted, trailing off as Seeker abruptly stiffened, raising her eyes to the ceiling.

"What is it?" Guyime asked her.

"Lissah," Seeker said, expression grim. The caracal had been dispatched to the tower's summit to keep watch whilst they gathered in the crypt. "She smells them. There are many. Every soul that once dwelt in this valley is rising from the lake."

Her warning was confirmed by the muted sound of alarmed voices echoing down the stairwell. "Stay here," Guyime told Lexius as the others all made for the steps. "There must be something, some clue, otherwise Ekiri couldn't have found it."

"But, won't all blades be needed?" Lexius protested, putting a hand to the Kraken's Tooth.

"You're the keenest mind I've encountered in a very long life," Guyime told him as he strode to the stairwell. "But also, perhaps, the worst swordsman. Your place is here. Keep looking and fetch me when you find it."

Emerging into the courtyard, he found the barricades had been only partially completed. Those on the breaches stood four feet high whilst the bracing of nailed-together timber at the gate was more substantial. Although standing taller than most men, the barrier still left an appreciable gap between its upper beams and the gate's arch.

"We've no time," Guyime told an anxious Anselm who had been engaged in loudly haranguing the labouring soldiers to nail more timbers in place. One glance over the barricade covering the nearest beach revealed an ugly and growing tide on the lakeshore. The dire-wights were struggling free of the water in a thick mass at the base of the isthmus, whilst dozens more splashed about amidst the moss-slick rocks at the keep's base. Whatever malign intelligence guided these things was evidently intent on assaulting them from all sides.

"Sergeant Tuhmel!" Guyime called out. The stocky soldier came quickly to his side, face beaded with sweat from both toil and well-justified fear. "Line up all the casks you can at the gatehouse barricade to create a parapet," Guyime told him. "Take half the company and work them in relays as they tire. They are to use their halberds at all times and make sure each man is wearing gloves. These things die when you crush their skulls and a single bite is fatal. Get to it, man!" he snapped when Tuhmel hesitated to cast a questioning look at Anselm. Receiving a nod from his lord, the sergeant ran off, shouting orders.

Guyime expected a prideful rebuke from Anselm regarding infringement of his authority, but instead the knight's attention seemed mostly fixed upon the entrance to the tower. It glowed with the light of the fire inside where Lothare still laboured to ease the pains of a dying squire.

"Your place is here," Guyime reminded him. "The men need to see their lord is not afraid."

"He saved my life," Anselm said, eyes lingering on the doorway. "More than once. My father used to say that, without a good squire, a knight is just a pampered fop in shiny plate." He laughed, bitter and short. "A man of great insight, my father, even more so when he'd had a few skinfuls of wine. He wasn't born to nobility, you see. He won it by dint of courage in arms, something neither he nor the true nobles ever forgot. Although born to title, I have truly been one of them. Elsinora didn't care, though. Nor did Galvin."

"You'd be best placed close to the gate, my lord," Guyime advised when Anselm lapsed into a reflective silence. "With your permission, the Stone Dogs shall oversee the breaches."

Anselm blinked and nodded, drawing his longsword then pausing to cast a frowning glance around the courtyard and the ragged walls of Blackfyre Keep. "This is a useless pile of stones, is it not, Captain?" He spoke without expectation of an answer, laughing again and shaking his head. "Strange I didn't see it before. I had such dreams of it. A castle of my own, far away from the sneers and scorn of the western nobles. I would have been a good lord to the people here; fair and just. Now, it appears they want to eat me."

"Destroy them all and the lands will be empty," Guyime said. "And good land is never wanting for tenants."

He strode off, beckoning to Seeker and the others. "Choose your spot," he told the Beast Charmer, nodding to the battlements. As she ran for the steps abutting the gatehouse, he resisted the impulse to remind her that every arrow had to count: he had never seen her miss.

"Ultria," he said, turning to Orsena. "If you would have a care for the eastward breach and I'll see to the west. Master Druid, abide in the courtyard and conserve your strength. If these barricades fall, we'll need your winds to cover a withdrawal to the tower."

Lorweth gave a pale-faced nod before forcing a grin. "A tight spot to be sure, your worship," he said. "Still, I'd wager you've known a few tighter, eh?"

"Save for the wrath of a mad god, no." Guyime attempted an encouraging smile, but from the way the druid took an involuntary backward step, deduced it resembled more the leering grimace of a grizzled tyrant steeped in death.

Orsena appeared more resolute as they moved to the rear of the tower, though he assumed inhuman strength did much to buttress the courage of one facing combat in battle for the first time. Still, there was some uncertainty in her bearing before they separated, a flexing of her hands as she clutched the hilt of the Conjurer's Blade. "There are…children amongst them?" she asked.

"All ages, all sizes." Seeing her hands twitch again he added, "They are not people any longer. They are not even beasts. They are worse. See only the evil that animates them and do not spare. If one gets past you, this keep will fall."

He watched her nod and stride off, then went to the south-facing breach. It was the narrowest of the gaps in the walls and therefore the most easily barred. Four men-at-arms waited at the barricade, faces stark with fear. "Get your gloves on," Guyime instructed one when he saw the man's hands smear sweat on the haft of his halberd. He stared at the soldier until he complied, then peered into the breach. "They can only come at you one at a time here. When you kill them, try to push the corpses back a ways so they don't pile up before the barricade."

The sweaty-palmed soldier promptly vomited on his half-donned gloves, much to the profane disgust of his comrades. "Shut your yap!" Guyime ordered, his voice the hard rasp that had once commanded thousands and ordered men flogged to death for ill-discipline. He paused to let their abrupt silence string out; it was good that they fear him more than they feared what was coming.

"If it looks as if the breach will fall," he said, placing a hand on the spewer's shoulder, "come fetch me at the eastern breach."

"Yes, my lord," the fellow breathed, a glimmer of hope rising in his eyes.

"Just a captain, lad."

He found the east-facing breach in a yet more aggravating state of disorder, the half-dozen men-at-arms stationed there exchanging fearful glances as they stood around in tense uncertainty. A few curt snaps of the Ravager's voice sufficed to set them in motion, trundling two carts up to the barricade to serve as a parapet and gathering a stack of wood-axes for secondary weapons.

Guyime chose the three most sturdy-looking soldiers to stand alongside him atop the carts, instructing the others to hand up the axes should their halberds break. He also made it clear in unmistakable terms that they were to take the place of any fallen comrades.

"And," Guyime added in a growl, eyeing the disturbed water around the rocks beyond the breach, "if any of you bastards are minded to run, the end I'll give you will make being taken by these creatures seem a mercy."

Chapter Eight

The Druid's Hour

The first dire-wight to struggle free of the water clambered over the rocks in a manner that resembled a deformed crab, skittering and sliding from one moss-covered boulder to another until it achieved the breach. The thing had been an adult when killed, but its skeletal appearance and part-rotted flesh made it impossible to discern gender, or anything else that might afford an identity. Had it been a fisherman? A shepherdess? Father or mother?

See only the evil, Guyime reminded himself, focusing on the wight's glowing green eyes as it flung itself at the barrier. By sheer dint of inhuman strength it dug its hands into the planking, stripping flesh from bone to gain purchase before hauling itself up, mouth gaping to issue the guttural hiss that appeared to be the only language permitted these creatures.

Guyime cleaved its head open with a single stroke of the sword, the green eyes blinking then fading to black as it fell away. "It's as simple as that," he told the soldiers at his side. "Why would a man fear such a simple task?"

Two more clawed their way up only moments later, a man and a woman. The soldiers' halberds hacked into their gaping faces, sending them tumbling atop the wight Guyime had killed. A group of four came next, a young woman accompanied by three small children who scampered up the barricade in a blur of chittering teeth and lashing, fleshless claws. Guyime sliced two in half with a deft sweep of the sword before stabbing it into the nose of the young woman as she hauled herself atop the barrier. One of the children, a tiny creature that couldn't have been more than four, latched itself to a soldier's halberd and scaled the haft to hurl itself at the man's face. Screams and blood erupted, the soldier falling from the cart, panicked hands trying to cast away the infant furiously biting his face and throat. One of the soldiers, also screaming, swung a wood axe to dislodge the child, propelling it into a high arc to land on the flagstones where it thrashed and hissed.

"Finish it!" Guyime shouted, a command which drew only blank stares from the men-at-arms. Cursing, he jumped from the cart and strode towards the gibbering wight, boot stamping down to pulp its skull. "This is not a time for mercy," he told them, pausing to regard the stricken soldier. The man's face was a ruin below the nose, his eyes very bright and wide amidst the red mess as he clutched hands to the gaping wound in his throat. Guyime finished him with a sword-thrust to the forehead.

"Any who die will come back," he told the man's silent, staring comrades before clambering back onto the cart. Scanning the breach and the rocks beyond, he counted twenty pairs of green eyes with more shimming into view as they emerged from the lake. From the base of the barricade came the chittering hiss of the two children he had cut in half, their separate parts scrabbling about in the dirt. Guyime raised his eyes from the obscenity of it and steeled himself for the next rush.

As he began hacking down more wights, he reflected on the increasing weight of the sword and the frustrating knowledge that, had Lakorath not been bound within its steel prison, he could have scythed through this entire horde in moments. *Cursed I am*, he thought, severing the spindly bone and gristle of an old man's neck, *but it always was a useful curse.*

In his days as a merely mortal man, combat had tended to be a brief, frenzied experience. Sieges, of course, were protracted affairs but the actual moments of violence they engendered would last minutes rather than hours. The onslaught against Blackfyre Keep, however, was anything but brief. He spent over an hour dispatching the hissing, clawing horde assailing the eastern barricade, refusing to surrender to the mounting aches setting a fire in his overworked muscles. Lulls came only when the pile of wight bodies grew so thick the others couldn't throw themselves at the soldiers atop the barrier. Once again, Guyime witnessed the guile of their foe as they turned their attentions to the bodies, shoving and dragging the corpses with such energy that limbs were wrenched loose of the gory mass.

"Shifting the slain aside so that they can get at us," the soldier at Guyime's side observed, voice breathless with fatigue. At Guyime's instruction, the soldiers had been rested at regular intervals, trading places with their comrades when they began to sag. Even so, the pace of killing took an increasing toll, and Guyime could tell many were fast approaching the point of exhaustion.

"Not aside," he said, watching one brutish-looking creature shove a dismembered head into the base of the barricade then drag a woman with a crushed skull into place alongside. More bodies were swiftly arranged into the pile, one atop another so that within moments the formed a mound a foot high.

"They're building a ramp." Guyime cast his gaze about the courtyard. He could hear the tumult of combat from the gate and the other breaches, but it seemed all were holding, at least for the moment. However, as these things seemed to share a common purpose, he knew those at the other points of attack would be following the same tactic.

"Fetch oil," he ordered the soldiers below the barricade. "And torches, we'll burn them…"

His words were swallowed by the loudest chorus of hissing and clacking from the wights yet. Turning, he saw a far greater mass of scrabbling bodies emerging from the water, whilst those in the breach drew into a tight cluster. It was clear to Guyime's battle-honed eye that what had gone before was but a preamble for a far more orchestrated assault.

The cluster of dire-wights in the breach charged without pause, ascending their ramp of flesh to hurl themselves at the top of the barricade, their hisses and chattering teeth creating a hideous parody of a war cry. It sufficed to unnerve one of the soldiers to the point of panic, the man dropping his halberd and leaping from the carts before the wights even reached them. Had he the time, Guyime would have cut the man down before he fled, but the onslaught closed upon him with inhuman speed.

All cohesion evaporated in the face of the assault, Guyime's sense of time and place lost in the maelstrom of leering, biting faces, lashing claws and the repeated spatter of unleashed gore as he swung the sword again and again. He only dimly heard the screams of the soldiers, some in defiance, others in the despair and terror of an ugly death. He became aware of the hard, unyielding wall pressing into his back and realised he had been pushed all the way across the courtyard to the tower's base. For a time he continued to fight with all the fury that had earned the Ravager such grim renown. Skull after skull split open as the Nameless Blade slashed and cut, the flagstones slicking with the dark fluids and grey brains of the dead. But even the Ravager at his worst was never immune to strain, and the frenzy of battle will only fuel a body for so long.

His arms finally gave out when he hacked through two skulls with the same stroke, the raging fire in his muscles sending a spasm through his entire being. Falling to his knees, he dragged air into his lungs in ragged gasps, casting a baleful eye at the wights now looming above, eyes burning brighter than ever.

A fitting end for the Ravager, he reflected, glancing down at the sword in his hand, still refusing to fall. Despite his strength being all but spent, he grasped the handle of the Nameless Blade with an irresistible firmness he knew wouldn't fade until the last glimmer of life had left his body. So many miles he had walked with this thing on his back, so many lives taken upon drawing it, but, since he began this search, also saved. The Ravager was dead, but he, the pilgrim who went in search of the Seven Swords, was not. "I…" he growled, a last flare of rage kindling in his chest, "…still have work to do."

Rage alone enabled him to stand, spittle flying from his lips as he roared defiance at the encroaching dead, determined to at least die standing. The wights were keen to oblige him, surging forward with claws outstretched, all mouths gaping wide…

When it struck, the gale was so fierce it stripped the skin from the first wights it touched. Flesh and grit stung Guyime's eyes, the courtyard turning into a hazy confusion of tumbling bodies and shredded detritus. Although shielded from the worst of it, the force still spun him about, sending him careening off the tower wall and rolling across the courtyard before it subsided.

"Your worship?" Guyime blinked the dirt from his eyes, revealing Lorweth's features staring down at him, drawn and pale. "Didn't do you an injury, I hope."

"None I'd punish you for," Guyime grunted, shifting to one knee then pushing himself upright. A glance at their surroundings revealed a sprawl of bodies, all smashed by the druid's gale. Although they were now just sacks of flesh housing broken bones, those wights with intact skulls still attempted to get at them, clawing pathetically at the ground in helpless bloodlust. Of the soldiers Guyime had stood alongside at the barricade, none survived, their corpses twitching as the emerald light began to glimmer in their eyes.

Looking to the breach they had fought so hard to defend, Guyime was surprised to find it empty, the lake waters beyond placid and undisturbed. It seemed that here, at least, their foe had exhausted their number. A upsurge of shouts and screams from the far side of the tower made it clear that this wasn't true of the entire keep, however.

"The Ultria," Guyime said, setting off at the plodding run his ache-wracked body allowed him. As they rounded the tower they came to the south-facing breach, finding but one soldier still at his post. The absence of armour-clad bodies at his side indicated his comrades had fled. Drawing closer, Guyime recognised the pale-faced youth as the one who had spewed in fear. He stared at Guyime with wide eyes and features flecked in corpse-muck, the blade of his halberd dark and glistening down to the hilt.

"One at time, Captain," he said, Guyime looking past him to see the breach beyond was choked with slain or twitching wights.

"There's no more to be done here," Guyime told him, gripping his shoulder. "Follow us now, lad."

Hurrying on, he cleared the side of the tower to see Orsena whirling amidst a throng of wights. The breach she defended was crammed with the green-eyed dead, a writhing and heaving mass that spilled ever more of their number into the courtyard. Guyime saw men-at-arms in the mob surrounding her, eyes glowing green. Even though the Ultria claimed plenty as she whirled, the Conjurer's Blade a streak of silver as it opened skull after skull with near surgical precision, Guyime knew that sheer weight of numbers would soon overwhelm her.

"Wait until I get her clear," he told Lorweth before hefting the Nameless Blade and plunging into the swarming wights. He made no effort to be sure of cleaving heads as he hacked his way to Orsena's side, chopping through legs and arms to clear a path.

"Hold!" he shouted as she whirled towards him, raising the sword in time to parry the arc of the Conjurer's Blade. As they met, the two swords chimed with unnatural volume, the sound far from musical but also powerful in the way it pained the ears. It also wrought a curious effect on the wights, freezing them in place, a strange, confused frown appearing on each grey, degraded face.

Keen to take full advantage of the distraction, Guyime took hold of Orsena's arm and dragged her from the throng, barreling the wights aside whilst the echo of the unnatural chime faded. The hissing, chattering chorus returned then, arms once again lashing bone-clawed hands as Guyime pressed Orsena to the tower wall.

"Master Druid!" he shouted, the words smothered by a vast shriek as Lorweth unleashed his storm.

This time the Mareth crafted a whirlwind rather than a mere gale. The swirling, ravening vortex gathered dozens of wights into its embrace, tearing them apart to litter the courtyard in bodily debris. Having blasted away those assailing Guyime and Orsena, the storm shifted to savage those cramming the breach. A dark, ugly fountain of fluid and matter rose as the whirlwind tore into the mass of dead. Black rain fell upon the keep, born of Lorweth's tempest ravaging its way through the breach to the lake where it raised a final shimmering blossom of clear water before subliming into nothing.

Guyime slipped and stumbled across gore-covered flagstones to find Lorweth slumped against the tower wall, held upright by the young soldier. The druid sagged with patent exhaustion, the face he revealed upon looking up at Guyime pale as frost, his eyes hollowed with fatigue.

"We're not yet done," Guyime told him with a grimace of regret. The tumult of unabated battle still came from the gatehouse where the fate of this keep would be decided.

"Then," Lorweth groaned, extending an arm which Orsena took, draping it over her shoulders, "we'd best not tarry, eh?"

Guyime led the way whilst the Ultria and the soldier half-dragged a stumbling Lorweth in his wake. Slain men-at-arms rose to bar their path, green eyes glowing as they swung their halberds, Guyime shouting with the effort of cutting them down.

He felt scant surprise at finding the scene at the gate a shambles. The barricade was a splintered wreck that only partially impeded the influx of wights, Anselm and only three surviving soldiers desperately attempting to hold back the tide of dead, retreating as they fought. A flurry of arrows arced down from the battlements to spear a dozen or more wights through the head, but no more followed. Guyime saw Seeker rapidly descending the steps beside the gatehouse, long-knife in hand and quiver empty, Lissah loping alongside. He noted that the other archers showed no indication to follow the beast charmer.

"Do you have the strength?" Guyime asked Lorweth.

The druid gave a dolorous glance at the soon-to-be-overwhelmed gate, blinking dulled eyes. "Got a breeze or two left, your worship," he said with a weak grin. "Can't get them all, though."

Guyime nodded and turned to Orsena. "If I fall, withdraw to the tower. Don't wait to seal the door."

From the hard glare she gave him he knew this was an instruction she would ignore but he had not the leisure to argue. "Rally to me, my lord!" he called out, rushing forward to take his place at Anselm's side. The knight had only two men-at-arms remaining now, his sword bloody to the hilt and the gleam of his armour concealed beneath a coating of wet grime.

"We have to hold the gate!" Anselm shouted back, delivering an overhead swing that split a rotund woman's head down to the neck.

"The gate is lost!" Guyime insisted, ducking under a slashing claw and skewering the skull of its owner. "And we can no longer hold the breaches. We must retire to the tower. We'll bar the door and await the dawn."

"As sound a plan as any, my lord," one of the soldiers advised, Guyime recognising Sergeant Tuhmel's heavy jaw beneath a mask of glistening dirt.

Anselm revealed a set of white teeth in a grimace of enraged frustration, voicing a hard shout as he brought his longsword down on yet another skull. "Very well," he grunted, standing back from the hissing throng to cast his voice at the battlements. "To the tower!"

As they turned and ran, Guyime saw that the archers stayed where they were, preferring the illusory security of their lofty perches, a decision that surely spelt their doom.

Lorweth raised his arms the moment Guyime and Anselm reached him. The gale the druid unleashed failed to match the fury of his eviscerating whirlwind but nevertheless possessed enough power to send every wight within the walls flat on its back.

"Get him inside!" Guyime told Orsena as the druid's winds died and he sagged between her and the young soldier. Seeker waited at the door for them, consenting to enter only at Guyime's insistent shout. He lingered until Orsena and the soldier dragged Lorweth inside quickly followed by Anselm and Tuhmel. The other surviving man-at-arms had delayed his retreat a second too long and been caught by Lorweth's gale, finding himself thrown into the mass of wights filling the gate. Before Guyime rushed inside and the others forced the makeshift door in place, he saw the man's arms flailing as he disappeared into the dark, thrashing mob, his screams mercifully brief.

Chapter Nine

The Spectre's Vigil

They buttressed the timbers on the door with every scrap of wood within the tower, Tuhmel retrieving a hammer and nails from somewhere to construct the haphazard arrangement while Guyime, Orsena and Anselm leant their strength to keep it closed. Once the last nail had been pounded into place the barrier shook and shuddered continually, creaking and groaning under the undaunted fury of the dire-wights outside.

"How many hours till dawn, d'you reckon, Captain?" Tuhmel asked, palming a melange of red grime and sweat from his brow.

Too many, Guyime didn't say. He put the hour at only marginally past midnight, meaning the dawn was a long way off. "We'll be counting corpses in the morning mist soon enough," he lied with gruff reassurance. "Still, be a good idea to check the water barrel, sergeant."

The man's heavy jaw worked as he fought to master his fear, eyes shading with the same expression Guyime had seen on many a soldier: the guilty relief that arises from surviving a battle that claims his comrades.

"My lads..." he began, voice dwindling quickly before he stiffened and moved to the water barrel.

"If you wouldn't mind?" Guyime said, turning to Orsena and gesturing at the door.

"It's beneath the dignity of an Ultria of Atheria to reduce herself to the role of door minder," she told him with arch sarcasm. Her humour faded quickly as a yet more intense bout of pounding sent an alarming shudder through the mishmash of timbers. Sighing, Orsena pressed her hands to the beams, muttering, "One of them bit me, you know." She nodded to her forearm which, as far as Guyime could tell, remained as pale and perfect as always.

"I felt it," she went on, frowning. "It hurt a great deal. But, as you can see, no blood, no marks. I do wonder, your highness, if it is actually possible for me to die, and I find that scares me more than any thought that has ever entered my head."

Various pointless reassurances, and a few somewhat cruel witticisms, came to mind as he regarded her downcast features. Even stricken by sorrowful reflection, her face retained the same near-absurd beauty that marked her as something beyond human, something that might grow to be monstrous should the demon in her blade ever claim purchase on her soul. But, then, that had also been true of him for many years now.

"Should we survive this," he said, "I've little doubt that this mission of ours will test that theory to its ultimate conclusion."

A smile ghosted across her lips. "Such rousing speeches you give, your highness. I can see why they made you a king."

Guyime grunted a very slight laugh. "I must confer with Lexius."

"That sound," she said, the humour slipping from her face. "When our swords met. What was that?"

"I don't know. I've never crossed swords with a cursed blade before."

"They heard it, the dead. It had some effect on them, made them hesitate."

"Then we can use it, and three blades clashing may produce something even more powerful. I'm sure Lexius may have a thought or two that may be relevant."

As he made his way to the stairwell leading to the crypt, he was distracted by the sight of Galvin's sweat-covered form. It was a testament to the squire's remarkable fortitude that he had clung to life for so long, but, judging by increasingly ragged breaths and the faltering heave of his chest, the end would come soon. Father Lothare sat at his side, continuing to press a damp, cooling cloth to the dying man's fevered brow. Galvin spoke in slurred, confused murmurs, his face a shade of grey that bore more than a passing resemblance to the ravening creatures outside.

"Will…" Galvin groaned, head lolling as he blinked unseeing eyes. "Will you hear my…unburdening, Father?"

"Of course I will, my son," Lothare assured him, taking the squire's hand. "We'll forgo the formalities, eh? Just speak your heart and know the Risen will forgive all."

"They…might," Galvin whispered. "But will *he?* Will she… Elsinora?"

The weight with which he spoke the name caused Guyime to pause. Much can be heard in the speaking of a single name; longing, loss, regret, devotion. Guyime heard it all now, as he had once heard it in his own voice when speaking of the wife he had lost to the church's flames.

"You'll make your peace with all," Lothare said. "In the High Realms."

"She'll know I failed..." Galvin's sagging features took on a sudden animation, guilt and fear adding a glimmer to the previously dulled eyes. "She'll blame herself. For indulging Anselm... for making me promise to keep him safe. But she need not, Father. I would have come even if...she hadn't wished it. But she wept so the day we left...wept for her hateful mother that set us on this path. Wept for Anselm and his blind devotion...wept for us. For the love we shared...and hid... I don't want her to weep, Father."

A soft exhalation drew Guyime's gaze to Anselm, standing nearby and staring at Galvin, eyes unblinking and face drained of emotion. It was clear he had heard every word.

"I have done...wrong, Father," Galvin pleaded, hands clutching at the sleeves of the priest's robe. "Betrayed my only true friend...the man I call brother. So many times... I wanted to tell him...but I feared what he would do. To himself...to her..."

Beset by a sense of intrusion, and seeing a dark glower begin to mar the knight's brow, Guyime turned away to descend the steps to the crypt. If Anselm chose to murder his squire it would, in truth, be a mercy.

At first glance he wondered if Lexius had fled the crypt and the keep, for the scholar was nowhere to be seen. A shuffling of fabric and scrape of metal on stone, however, drew him to the far end of the chamber. He found Lexius on his hands and knees, using the point of the Kraken's Tooth to chip away at the base of the oldest tomb.

"It was just a slight misalignment," the scholar explained, glancing up at Guyime before resuming his labour. "And the dimensions of this sarcophagus are fractionally larger than the others. Everything else in this crypt is striking in its uniformity. There had to be a reason."

Sinking to his haunches, Guyime saw that Lexius had succeeded in chipping away sufficient stone to reveal a narrow but discernible gap between the tomb's base and the flagstones. He glimpsed only blank darkness beneath the opening but it also exuded a musty redolence tinged with the tell-tale acrid sting he knew all too well.

"A tomb beneath a tomb," he said, drawing the Nameless Blade and joining its unyielding steel to Lexius's efforts. Several moments of labour succeeded in widening the gap but, even with the cursed blades, it was clear digging an aperture of sufficient size required days of work.

Shifting his attention to the sarcophagus, Guyime ran a hand over its ancient stone flank before trying an experimental shove. He expected little and assumed he would have to fetch Orsena to move the thing, so started in surprise when it pivoted an inch to the left, exposing yet more of the gap.

"It's not a tomb," Lexius said with a sigh of self-recrimination. "It's a door."

Together they pushed at the sarcophagus, revealing an opening of ample dimensions to accommodate entry. Taking a torch, Guyime dipped it into the gloomy orifice, the flickering light playing over a set of heavily cobwebbed steps descending into a dusty void. He was no stranger to dark and forbidding places, but this one gave him pause. Even without Lakorath's demonic insight he was familiar enough with the unique prickling to the skin and churning of the guts that bespoke a spectral presence below.

"I should fetch the others," Lexius said, squinting into the shadows.

"Orsena's strength is needed to hold the door and, if there's a sword to be found here, it would be best if Seeker is kept from it."

"In case she's tempted to claim it, I assume?"

"Quite." Guyime snorted a breath and started down the steps. "She would endure any burden to save Ekiri, but I'll not abide her suffering the weight of a cursed blade."

Although a dense matrix of cobwebs covered the steps, it was clear to him that a channel had been carved through it not so long ago. The thickness of the grey, gossamer curtains above his head indicated that whoever had walked this passage recently was not so tall as he.

"Whatever lies here," he said, stooping under a low vaulted ceiling, dusty tendrils hissing in the torchlight, "Ekiri already found it."

"Guided by the Crystal Dagger, no doubt," Lexius added. "It seems her demon knows more than yours, my lord."

A caustic joke regarding Lakorath's wealth of ignorance rose then faded from Guyime's lips. It was certainly true that, for so ancient a being, the demon repeatedly displayed a remarkable lack of knowledge. However, Guyime knew this to result mostly from indifference, and the insight Lakorath did choose to share was often copious and in fact a fraction of the huge well of knowledge he possessed. If the demon inhabiting the Crystal Dagger did know more, it made it a fearsome adversary indeed.

A few steps on the low ceiling rose as the short passage gave way to a far larger chamber. The prickle to Guyime's skin increased as he entered, even though the shadows remained undimmed. The torchlight flickered on ancient, rough-hewn foundations upon which Blackfyre Keep had been built. They formed a circle of wide pillars around a central depression. Moving deeper, Guyime's torch revealed a coffin in the centre of the chamber. This was no finely crafted tomb like those above, but a plain box of old, part-rotted wood, yet its occupant was far from decayed.

The figure lay in knightly armour that shone bright in the torch's flame, unmarred by spider's web or dust. Gauntleted hands rested on the breastplate, beneath which there lay a sword. Its ancient design was evident to Guyime's educated eye; a single-edged blade, slightly curved forward from a bronze hilt, guard and handle. It was a sword seen on fragments of pottery from the legendary days before the rise of Valkeris. This, he had no doubt, was the Necromancer's Glaive.

Yet, it was not this mythical object that most captured his attention, but the face of its owner, for it was a face he knew.

"Ihlene," Guyime breathed. Although her features showed no sign of life, she remained the image of the woman he had last seen dying on Saint Maree's field, hands clutched to a gushing wound in her belly. Her jet black hair had the same sheen, her features strangely serene in their aquiline beauty, so at odds to the fierce woman he had known, a beauty enhanced rather than marred by the scar on her forehead.

"You know this woman?" Lexius asked as Guyime raised then withdrew a tentative hand from her face.

"This is Lady Ihlene Hardeysa," he replied, a faint smile playing across his lips despite the impossibility of it all. "The Steel Thorn Rose, they called her. She was at my side…the Ravager's side throughout all his battles, and glorious was she in her fury. She died at Saint Maree's field. That enchanted painting in Orsena's Galleria did a fair job of depicting it."

"Then how can she be here, holding that sword…?"

The scholar's voice dwindled as a new sound filled the chamber, a soft, sibilant scrape over the stones punctuated by a rattle Guyime recognised as bone on granite. It seemed to come from all around. Guyime and Lexius whirled to cast their torchlight about the chamber, seeing only wisps of fluttering cobwebs. The sound abruptly stopped then, leaving an interval of utter silence until it was broken by a voice that was more a dusty breeze.

"Is that you, sire?"

Despite its strangeness, despite its plainly unnatural origin, Guyime knew this voice. The cadence of it, the kindness of it, unmistakable even now. Slowly, he turned, bringing the torch round to illuminate a figure crafted from the detritus of this tomb. Cobwebs and dust swirled to form limbs, torso and neck, atop which there sat a head of sorts. The dirt-flecked gossamer arranged itself to form a face, although Guyime could see the age-brown bone and teeth of a skull and jaw behind it. The cobweb mask shifted and twitched until it settled into another face he knew.

"Lorent…" Guyime took a step towards the thing before faltering to a halt. For a second he could only stare at this obscene spectre, this parody of perhaps the only man he had ever honestly named a hero. "You…" He stammered, swallowed and forced the words from his lips. "You came then, as you always said you would. You came to claim Blackfyre Keep."

"I did, sire. And brought my love to be my lady." Lorent's ghostly arm cast floating motes into the still air as it gestured to Ihlene's uncorrupted body. "See how beautiful she is. Also, how still." The shifting, barely substantial face formed into a expression of boundless sorrow. "Strange, is it not, sire, how our ambitions came to nothing in the end? You won a kingdom only to cast it away. I won her heart, only to cradle her as she lay dying. She told me, you know. Before her last breath. She told me she loved me..."

Lorent's breeze-like voice subsided as he lost himself in a reverie of the dead but un-decayed woman in the coffin. Guyime didn't want to think how many years his friend's ghost had spent in this endeavour, how long he had lingered alone and heartbroken in this hollow in the earth.

"The sword, Lorent," he prompted. "I must know about the sword."

"It's a vile thing, sire. Worse even than that blade you found in Sallish. A terrible, cursed thing... I uncovered it here, in the bowels of this ruin I thought might make a home. Old tales of Orwin Blackfyre and his many dark deeds led me to it. A blade that could raise the dead, so the old folk hereabouts told me. In the madness of my grief, I thought it would raise her. I was a fool, sire. The worst of fools..."

Lorent's ghost shifted, the cobwebs and dust blossoming into a cloud then reforming into the sight of a kneeling man, a gossamer hand playing over Ihlene's unmoving face. "The creature within the blade whispered to me, made promises... all lies, but I so wanted to believe. So I took up the sword, and called upon the demon to restore Ihlene to me, and he did. It banished the corruption that had marred her corpse, made her whole again, but not alive. The woman that climbed from this coffin was but a beauteous corpse, eyes glowing with green malice, set on the slaughter and cruelty that is the delight of the thing that raised it.

"I knew my sin, then, sire. I knew what I had done. All the madness slipped away as I beheld Ihlene as she never was. By will alone I contained the demon in the sword. Though it railed at me, punished me with many agonies, still I held it in check and sealed the tomb so that neither it nor I, nor Ihlene, would ever escape this place. With a final effort of will, I sank the cursed blade into my own chest, lay upon Ihlene's body and pressed it into her hands just as all life left me.

"Here we lay, entwined together for years uncounted, whilst my body withered to bone and then dust and she, imbued with the sword's malice, remained unchanged. This was our fate in the end, her a corpse and I a ghost, for the old tales had some truth to them. A witch did once curse this keep, angered by the cruelties of Orwin Blackfyre. His ghost still clings to these stones but it is a withered, barely aware thing. For that is the destiny of those cursed to exist beyond death: bereft of feeling we slip into the shadows to become a flicker on the edge of mortal vision. I, however, have not withered, for Ihlene sustains me. Her beauty and my own despair are my sustenance. What worse fate than to linger in this place forever, an eternal witness to all I lost?"

"Until Ekiri came," Guyime said. "The girl with the crystal dagger. She came here, did she not?"

"I did not hear her name, for she spoke with a voice not her own. A demon voice. It was plain to me that she had failed where I had succeeded, her will had not contained the demon in the blade. But I couldn't fault her for it. I felt the power of that demon, Kalthraxis it named itself, and doubt even you could have contested it, sire."

Lorent's ghost shifted again, spectral hands playing over the Necromancer's Glaive. "The thing in this feared it too, I could sense it. What manner of Infernus-spawn can instill terror in another demon? Kalthraxis laughed at it, taunted it. 'Thou wilt be of service, brother,' it told the Glaive. 'Rejoice in the knowledge that, for but once in thine entire miserable existence, I shall bless thee with the gift of importance.' Then it laughed… All the horrors I have witnessed, and yet that laugh chills even my absent heart."

"What…" Lexius began, coughing before managing to phrase his question. A stalwart soul at most times, it seemed the act of conversing with a ghost sufficed to unnerve him. "What did it do? How did it awaken the sword's power?"

"Why, merely by touching it, good sir," Lorent replied. "That is all. There was a command in that touch, I could feel it. The demon in the Glaive was as bound by its will as that girl. The power it unleashed pained me, for it was the touch of death given substance, a great blossoming of it like an oil-soaked beacon fire surging at the first kiss of the torch."

From far above there came a sudden, indistinct sound. Guyime couldn't tell if it was a shout, a clamour of combat, or the barred door to the tower finally giving way. "It must be mastered," he said, settling a steady, determined eye on the Necromancer's Glaive.

"My lord…" Lexius cautioned as Guyime reached out to grasp the cursed blade.

"To contain the demon, the sword needs a wielder," he said. "This much I know. If it's my fate to carry two cursed blades, so be it."

His finger barely made contact with the Glaive's gleaming bronze pommel before a vibrating thrum of energy seized his arm and cast it away. Spun by the force of it, Guyime collided with a foundation pillar, grunting as pain coursed its way from his limb to his chest where it flared briefly before fading.

"The curse that binds the demon will not tolerate the sharing of a mortal soul, sire," Lorent's ghost told him, his barely substantial features taking on a grim aspect. "An un-cursed hand must wield this blade."

Guyime and Lexius exchanged glances as another dim but alarming noise echoed from above. "Seeker or Lorweth," Lexius said, a potent glimmer of shame showing in his magnified eyes.

"No," Guyime growled back, struggling to his feet.

"There's no other way, my lord. A mortal hand must take up this blade, a hand not already cursed to carry one of the Seven Swords."

"Then let it be mine," a soft, toneless voice stated. Guyime's eyes snapped towards the sight of Anselm emerging from the shadows. The knight's gaze was fixed upon the ancient weapon lying in Ihlene's hands, his expression mingling utter despair with implacable resolve.

"You don't know what this is, boy," Guyime told him.

"I've heard enough to know it's the only way to save us." Anselm approached the coffin with an unhurried assurance, Guyime seeing no sign of fear or hesitation in his bearing. "So, Captain," the knight added in a low murmur, "this is what you came for. Father Lothare tried to warn me there was a hidden purpose in your loyalty. It appears you owe me some coin, having obtained it by false pretences."

"You do not command me, demon," Guyime reminded him, although, as he continued to stare helplessly at the knight's agonies, the direness of their predicament became stark. There was nothing to be done but flee this keep and forsake the sword. The vale of Stillwater Lake would forever be a cursed place roamed by the ravenous dead.

It was then that Lorent's ghost began to gather yet more substance to itself. Dust and detritus formed a short-lived maelstrom in the confines of the subterranean tomb, swirling to add matter to the shifting apparition. When it cleared Guyime found that Lorent's face had become almost a mirror image of the handsome, sorrowful man Guyime remembered. It stared at him for a heartbeat, a sad smile playing over its dusty lips then, taking on a frown of grim determination, it surged forward to envelop Anselm's now-twitching form.

The knight's struggles had diminished by then, subsiding as his soul lost its contest with the demon in the Glaive. But, as Lorent's dusty spectre covered him, his body began to jerk with even greater animation than before.

Now, that's a true contest, Lakorath said. *The ghost is a far more formidable spirit than the boy, it seems.*

"Who's winning?" Guyime asked, continuing to watch the knight flail and gibber, the green glow of the sword in his hands flickering like a guttering torch.

Can't really tell. Still, it's all providing a decent distraction. We should be able to get clear of here without drawing too much notice.

"We're going nowhere." Hearing a fresh bout of indistinct noise from above, Guyime reached over his shoulder to draw the Nameless Blade, finding the blue glow of the steel brighter than ever. "We still have work to do."

Chapter Ten

The Cursed Knight

He told Lexius to stay with Anselm and hurriedly climbed free of the underground tomb, hurrying to scale the steps from the crypt to the tower. He found it littered with a dozen or more slain dire-wights, each one neatly decapitated. Orsena stood amongst the collection of heads and bodies, the Conjurer's Blade shimmering in her hand. He saw black blood disappear into the glowing steel as the demon inside drank its fill.

Seeing Guyime, Orsena wiped a spatter of gore from her face, offering a half-smile as she hefted her sword. "She likes it when I dance," she said.

The humour abruptly fled her features when a thunderous, discordant thumping sounded from above. It was, Guyime knew, the sound of many bodies falling onto the upper floor, meaning the ant-like mass of wights ascending the tower had now reached its summit. Within seconds, they tumbled down the stairs in an ugly, writhing mob. Seeing the energy with which they lashed their clawed hands and chattered their hissing mouths, Guyime sensed an even greater pitch to their bloodlust.

The Glaive calls for help from its minions, Lakorath explained. He let out a disdainful sigh as Guyime levelled the Nameless Blade and charged towards the base of the steps. *Wights, they always taste so foul.*

The first stroke cleaved through four wights at the waist, the next transforming them into chunks of twitching meat upon the floor. Guyime had none of Orsena's artistry and went about the task with a warrior's fury. He swung the sword again and again without pause or rest, all the aches that marked his age during Lakorath's enforced silence now vanished. Corpse-bile and congealed blood rose in a fountain to paint the walls whilst the sword described a ceaseless, glowing arc. Eventually, the sheer weight of dismembered bodies forced him back, the wights bursting free of the stairwell like guts from a split belly.

Guyime whirled, scything down a dozen with a single blow, but there were so many. One managed to latch a clawed hand to his arm, fleshless bones tearing at his sleeve to score the flesh beneath. A twist of the Nameless Blade lopped off its arm and head in short order, but the distraction allowed more to get past him.

A rush of displaced air followed by a loud boom put a ringing in Guyime's ears. Turning, he saw a new creature had entered the fray. It was a parody of a human figure, standing close to seven feet tall, consisting of a torso and limbs but no head. As it swung an arm into the mass of wights, crushing flesh and bone like damp twigs, Guyime saw that the limb was composed entirely of fractured stone.

Body parts flew as the creature hurled itself into the thick of the wights, stone arms blurring to wreak havoc. Guyime saw Orsena standing amidst a patch of floor that was bare down to the earth, the flagstones presumably having been torn up to craft her latest sculpture. She stared at the marauding creation with stern, unwavering focus, guiding its path of destruction. Yet, even so mighty a conjuration couldn't hold back this tide. The wights leapt upon the stone beast, mobbing it to shatter teeth and bone as they attempted to tear its unyielding flesh. It smashed and crushed with ferocious abandon but the weight of flesh upon it eventually brought it down. The wights stripped skin from their denuded flesh as they forced limbs into the gaps between the creature's stones, rending them apart.

Hearing a gasp from Orsena, Guyime turned to see her face bunching frustration. "Apparently, even demon magic has limits," she told him.

With her creation shattered the last obstacle had been removed from the path of the inrushing dead. Yet, now that victory was at hand, a strange indecision gripped them. Instead of hurling themselves at the living, they halted, twitching and jerking as the green glow in their eyes flickered, much like the guttering of the Glaive in the tomb below.

It appears the ghost is putting up a good fight, Lakorath said. *Although, I'd say the odds are still against him.*

"Back!" Guyime shouted to Orsena, both of them retreating to stand before Father Lothare and Galvin. Somehow the squire still clung to life, even attempting to rise and reach for his halberd, though he only managed a soft touch to the haft before collapsing into a senseless slumber.

Father Lothare hefted his gnarled walking stick and placed himself between Guyime and Orsena. Sergeant Tuhmel and the young soldier from the southern breach took their place on Guyime's right whilst Seeker and Lorweth positioned themselves to Orsena's left. Lissah crouched between beast charmer and druid, fangs bared and back arched.

"Any more winds left, Master Druid?" Guyime asked Lorweth, drawing a very faint chuckle from the grey-faced druid.

"Just a couple, your worship." He raised his hands in readiness, pausing when Guyime shook his head.

"Wait until they charge," he said, eyeing the dithering, gibbering wall of dead before them. The wights filled the chamber now, more thronging the steps beyond, all staggering about with the emerald light fluttering in their eyes.

"Always best to strike when the prey is distracted," Seeker said.

Guyime's gaze shifted to the door, still barred by their ramshackle construction of nails and wood. "Ultria," he said to Orsena, "can you transform that quick enough for us to get out?"

She took a moment to study the barrier, grimacing a little as the Conjurer's Blade flickered in her hand. "She'd rather craft something from all these sundered bones," she said, "but yes, it can be done."

"Master Druid," Guyime drew the sword back, tensing for the rush. There was no telling when the wights would regain their bloodlust and he had a sense they would have only seconds to achieve this. "If you could endeavour to carve us a path. Seeker, Father Lothare, see to the squire…"

He trailed off when a new animation rippled through the wights, each one taking on a rigid, arched-back pose, the light in their eyes glowing brighter than ever, building so that it seemed that a green fire blazed in every skull. Then, as one, they burst. The head of every wight exploded in a blossom of verdant iridescence, the combined flare of it forcing Guyime to avert his eyes, raising an arm to shield himself from the gritty blast of fragmented bone.

When he looked again the wights lay in a thick carpet of unmoving flesh, other lifeless cadavers slithering down the gore caked mass choking the stairwell. No limbs twitched and no sound came save the tick and slap of bile and blood dripping from the ceiling.

Footsteps echoed from below as a figure climbed the steps from the crypt. To Guyime's eyes, Sir Anselm Challice had contrived to age a decade in the scant moments since he left him in the tomb. He also appeared to have gained an inch in height, although Guyime felt that to be due to the knight's changed posture. His back was straighter and his gaze keener, also coloured by a knowledge that went far beyond his years. His longsword was sheathed at his side and in his hand he held the Necromancer's Glaive, the blade now emitting a far more muted green glow.

He spared the mass of bodies only the briefest glance before approaching them, moving with a purposeful surety as he picked his way through the corpses. His gaze was fixed on Galvin, eyes narrowed and mouth set in a hard line. The squire was still lying in his insensate sleep, although Guyime perceived a slight lessening in the greying pallor of his skin. Also, the ugly dark tendrils of corruption that had snaked out from under the bandage on his neck were gone now.

"Father Lothare," Anselm said, his voice jarring in its soft, sibilant quality, so different from his usually cultured and earnest tones. "It will be your sad duty to report to the king and the church that Sir Anselm Challice and most of his men fell defending Blackfyre Keep from a rebel army making use of vile magics. You will convey this man home and place him in the care of Lady Elsinora Hardeysa. Tell her this was Sir Anselm's dying wish."

Lothare's features were heavy with reluctance, for it was a sworn duty of a priest to speak no falsehood. Nevertheless, he replied with a grave and silent nod.

"Now then, Captain," Anselm said, shifting his gaze to Guyime. "Our scholarly friend tells me you are embarked upon a very interesting mission…"

"What will you tell the church?"

"What that fine young knight asked me to tell them," Father Lothare said, securing the chain on the cart's tailboard. Galvin lay on the bed of the cart, wrapped in blankets and drugged to prevent him waking, at Anselm's instruction. He hadn't come to bid priest or squire farewell, preferring to lend his labour to piling the copious dead atop the pyre now blazing on the isthmus. The dire-wights remains were void of all life, but consigning them to the flames still seemed a wise precaution.

Lothare paused to afford Guyime a look of prolonged and careful scrutiny. Finally, he sighed and said, "I think it best if the truth of what transpired here remains unspoken and unrecorded. Should the bishops learn of the Seven Swords they might be roused to unwise actions, yet more so if they were also to learn that the Ravager still walks this earth."

Guyime raised an eyebrow at that, surprised more by the fact that the urge to cut the priest down failed to rise in his breast.

"Your voice carried well from the crypt," Lothare explained. "To think I journeyed beside the worst of kings and never suspected. I knew you had a hidden motive for coming here, but this..." He trailed off, shaking his head, hard judgement and self-recrimination writ large in his face. Still Guyime felt no desire to kill him. Perhaps because he had stood so resolute throughout it all, or because he saw no true malice in this priest where once it would have been all he allowed himself to see.

So he merely shrugged and said, "That's dangerous knowledge to carry, father."

"All knowledge is dangerous, your highness."

Lothare allowed his gaze to linger a fraction longer then moved to the front of the cart, taking his place at the yoke alongside Tuhmel and the young soldier. All the horses and oxen had been slaughtered by the wights and they had no other means of conveying Galvin's bulky personage away from the vale.

"Let's be about it, my sons," Lothare said, lending his weight to the yoke and setting the cart in motion. "It may be cursed no longer, but the divine guidance of the Risen tells me it would be best not to loiter in sight of this keep."

Mercy, my liege? Lakaroth asked as the cart trundled away. *How uncharacteristic for the Ravager, the great persecutor of all priests.*

Guyime watched the cart until it crested the western rise and disappeared from view. "You were never just my burden, were you?" he asked the demon. "You were my leash. The muzzle on a raging monster that might have murdered all the world."

I suppose, Lakorath mused. *In a way.*

"Why? Is it not your nature to delight in destruction?"

It is my experience that mere destruction is ultimately an empty amusement. I find my delights come in many and varied forms. Most of them, I must confess after a very long span of existence, have arisen in the comparatively short time I have journeyed with you. Besides, I am not your slave compelled to fulfil your whims, be they murderous or benign. He fell silent for a short time and when he spoke again the demon's voice was laced with the taunting, barbed tone Guyime knew so well. *So, you missed me then?*

"But you don't fully know what the purpose of the Seven Swords is, sire?" The knight's use of this honorific, together with his steady, intent gaze and softened voice, both disconcertingly familiar, made Guyime wonder if the soul he conversed with was in fact Sir Anselm Challice.

"I know that fulfilling it will banish the curse that binds us to these blades," Guyime replied. "That alone makes this mission worthwhile."

"And if that purpose should prove dire, what then?"

The impression of conversing with Lorent rather than Anselm grew yet stronger. Lorent had never shied from posing difficult questions, although always with the expected deference. In the two days since they began their trek away from Blackfyre Keep, Guyime had refrained from asking the knight about his struggle with the demon inhabiting the Necromancer's Glaive. His one allusion to the subject had been met with a dark glower and resentful grimace that was all Anselm, for Lorent's manner was never so churlish. It was clear that the ghost of his former comrade had aided in mastering the demon, but had it been banished? And how much of Lorent, or Anselm remained? Guyime suspected the knight himself wasn't sure.

"Then it will remain unfulfilled," Guyime told him simply. "Wherever this journey leads, I made a promise to Seeker that Ekiri would be returned to her. If nothing else, I'll see that done."

"A worthy quest then."

"I believe so. One I will be honoured to undertake with you, if you're willing."

"So, I have a choice then?"

Guyime inclined his head to the others seated around the campfire. They had taken a south-easterly course away from the keep, guided by the map. Although it had once again become a confused jumble of swirling lines, most of them arced in this direction. The country was pleasing to the eye, rolling hills and well maintained fields dotted by farmsteads and villages. The people they encountered proved neither hostile nor welcoming, for who would not be suspicious of travellers from the cursed vale?

They made camp atop a gentle slope a full day's march from Blackfyre Keep. Conversation was muted, since Lorweth's fatigue had not fully lifted. Seeker had fallen to silent, frowning introspection, eyes lacking focus as she stroked a sleeping Lissah in her lap. Orsena and Lexius did consent to speak, but their softly spoken words were addressed to the spirits inhabiting their swords.

"These people follow my path for their own reasons," Guyime told Anselm. "I do not compel them, nor could I if I wished it, for they are all powerful. As are you, my lord."

Anselm looked away, his hand slipping to the hilt of the Necromancer's Glaive. He had found a sheath to fit it amongst the slain, his longsword he now carried on his back. Guyime could see a meagre glow emitting from the edge of the Glaive's scabbard and knew whatever lay within its steel was speaking in Anselm's mind. Again, Guyime refrained from asking questions. Bearing a cursed blade was never an easy task and he nursed a growing suspicion that this knight would find it harder than most.

"We..." Anselm began then paused, a flicker of annoyance passing across his face before he went on. "I will go with you, sire."

"I think I'd prefer if you just continued to call me Captain," Guyime told him, rising from the fire. "I haven't been a king for a very long time."

He unfurled the map as he wandered away from camp, moving to a vantage point that afforded a view of the southward landscape. He hoped the enchanted chart might consent to offer some insight when they were well clear of the keep and its lingering ghosts, but all he saw was yet more indistinct coiling of faint lines.

A simple solution would be to pick a direction and walk until these scribbles make sense, Lakorath opined, sensing Guyime's mounting frustration. *Of course, that might take years.*

"I wonder if this is some design of the demon in the Crystal Dagger," Guyime mused. "To craft a trap like that, Kalthraxis must be a demon of considerable abilities, and cunning."

At mention of that name the sword jerked on Guyime's back. It was very different from the usual thrum or vibration. Instead this was a convulsive reflex born of stark, unalloyed fear. He could feel it through the long silence that followed, Lakorath's abject, near panicked welling of terror.

Guyime said nothing, waiting for the sword and the demon to calm. When he spoke next, Lakorath's voice was as controlled and bare of emotion as Guyime had ever heard it. *That is the name of the demon in the Crystal Dagger?*

"Yes. Lorent learned it when Ekiri came here. You know this…?"

Don't say it again! Lakorath's fearful anger lashed at him. *Names have power, as I've told you countless times.*

"As you wish." Guyime drew the Nameless Blade, setting the blade against his palm as he watched blue glow swirl over the steel with far more animation than was typical. "Who or what is it?" he asked. "This demon that scares you so."

You recall the Mad God? A ragged bitter, sigh came from Lakorath then, laden with dark recollection. *This one is far worse. But at least now I have an inkling of where this journey will take us, my liege. You should burn that map. It won't help you now. Our adversary used it to lure you to the keep, meaning it can never again be trusted. Besides, I know where we need to go.*

"And where is that?"

Where I was enticed into this miserable realm of mortals and their endless, petty struggles. Where I was led like the most dull-witted goat into a baited trap. Where I was placed in this sword. We need to head south to the far reaches of the Axuntus Nuarem, where lies a region known as the Sorrow Sea.